BOYGOD

The Preface

In regards to me. I was born in the Philippines in 1993. For ten and a half years, I played under the heat of a smiling sun, and swam the torrents of a grinning rain. But it would be unjust for me to complain; childhood was more than generous. I used time leisurely with friends, received a private school education, and had gadgets and toys less fortunate children would immediately sell to ease their family's hunger. I lived under a roof where Mother took care of me and my two sisters with selfless hands. Father was an over-seas Filipino worker for most of my boyhood, yet his love was never distant. I was too young then to understand how it was to be alone; a life he lived until we moved to the United States with him in 2004.

In regards to you. To have a greater understanding of the universe I set myself to create, this must be the first to be read.

I don't create my characters, I meet them.

And so, I will begin with the person I think I spend the most time with, and that, is myself: a student of film, literature, and philosophy, a teacher to children, a friend to many, a loved one to few, but always, a stranger to every single one of you.

For you,
who deserves more than my universe can ever give.

                                        From me,
   who deserves every consequence for all that I've done.

Heat. Seething, hovering above the grey sand. This is so stupid. You're right there, behind the horizon, but I can't feel you. Why are you so far away?

Look at me. Don't look down—! Cause I can't see your eyes through the blur of this heat. Seething, seething, hovering, these red units of Hurt. We're in a desert stretching so far and a mile beyond that. You're that far, and I need your hand. I need your hand. I walk endlessly to nowhere just to get to you.

Because I want to be with you. I want to be with you. I want to be with you. Why can't I be with you? Why can't I clear my sight of the sky of blue, and instead cover it with your shoulders pressed against my red, puffy eyes, as you hold me in your arms—oh, no. Don't let it take me. Make it stop now. Make it stop. Red is spreading. I don't know what to do. I don't know how to end it. Squeeze it out of my eyes. Squeeze it out of my eyes. It's trying to play with me, these black lines. Black, black, bolt like black. Kill me. It burns, this red hurt... I don't want to see it... I don't want to see Hurt anymore...

I love you. Do you love me too? Please, don't be the feeling that strangles the neck before caressing the cheeks. Please, say that you love me too—because my nightmare is about to rip me apart... again... but you... you... you... you...

... are too far away to do... anything.

A Necessary Letter for My and Dy

I know you're both willing listeners. And your son is
in great need to say something.

Midnight it was when the *defining* nightmare of my
childhood returned at nine years old. You both had a
traumatic verbal fight again earlier that day. I told
Miel and Yanie that it was okay, but it was never okay.
My crying was loud, and I couldn't stop it. I opened
the door to a congested hallway lit by a yellow bulb.
Light snuck in as I crept my way in your dark room.

"*Anong nangyari? Bakit ka umi-iyak. Midnight na!*
(What happened? Why are you crying? It's midnight!),"
you said with a soft and exhausted voice.

"Mommy, I... I..." I couldn't tell you how I felt.
It was you! *How could a little boy tell you, his mom,
that he thinks she's wrong?* You stripped off your
blanket and slowly approached me. I wanted to scream
at you because of all the fights and the hate, and the
sadness I had put up with. At the time, I didn't know
that you too felt the same way as I feel now. It's
just the way our minds work. It gets frustrated, it
gets mad, but it loves so much—it loves so well.

"*Meron po akong napanaginipan na ang layo nyo* (I
had a dream that you were so far away). *Nasa desert
ako... tapos ang init-init... ng sand* (I was in the
desert... and the sand... was so hot). *May mga black
lines na nasa muka ko, nakikita ko kayo... sa other
side... pero every time I take another step... lumalayo
kayo* (There were black lines in front of my face. I
can see you... at the other side... but every time I
take another step... you go farther away)."

"*Breathe. Mag-hinga ka lang. Breathe... Anong
nangyari?* (Breathe. Just breathe... Breathe... What
happened?) Did you pray tonight?" you asked me.

"Mommy, I... I... always..." I sobbed like the baby
I was, like the baby I am. *How could I tell the both
of you that the fights are hurting us?* My mouth was
holding saliva, my nose was clogged with mucus, and my
eyes were almost empty. I was speechless. You cradled

me to sleep as you, Dy, came from the living room couch, having been woken up by my yelp. Still, Miel and Yanie were undisturbed—as it should be. I failed to speak a word of what I thought was wrong and instead fell asleep with you both holding me. *I'm sorry mom and dad for keeping you up. I've never been a child. I don't know what I am; no clue what I'm doing.*

But the same nightmare kept returning for three nights straight. With no warning, something in my head held on to my tongue and spilled itself full-force. That was when I finally told both of you how your little boy's big feelings were affected so much when he hears yelling all day and night. Funny... yelling once made me hurt and cry, but only yelling now can calm me down.

Now I'll tell you something not so funny. Three years ago, after the break-up with Emily, my mind fought a total-emotional war against the world. Right then and there, my universe and the world outside my head exchanged their horrors while I was caught in between. And the boy in me, your honest son, used his pen in hand to respond with an absolute cleansing ~~none of us were ready for~~. I. wasn't ready for. I know, I haven't told you yet until now. I'm dearly, so sincerely sorry that I still don't know what I'm doing with this life you gave me. I tried to make sense of it and this is what came out; journal-entries of the most extreme of moments, written tired and inebriated, edited kinda clearheaded (I think).

My and Dy, this is the psychology of your loving and caring, still *natututong anak* (learning child). *Mahal na mahal ko po kayo* (I love you very much).

Respectfully yours,

L.A.

P.S. I want you to understand why hurting as you read my la, la, land is okay. And almost. necessary.

BOYGOD

"Are you just going to call Rebecca and have her bring the money back? Okay... I'm totally screwed..." she said to me almost crying.

"Why's that?" I asked.

"I mess up all the time. I'm going to get blamed for this."

"It was my fault as a leader. I'll take care of it. You have enough going on..."

"What am I supposed to say when I get a call about this?"

"Tell management it was something small," I suggested.

"I don't know..."

"Ayla, you need to relax. It can be fixed. You're fine... I'm the one in trouble." Stressed person, I wish I could help you more.

"Thanks."

Why is this conversation from work still ringing in my head? I open my hellish eyes. Black room. Black blinds. ***Ring! Ring!*** My shoulder strains as it reaches my phone from above the cabinet. *Why is Cait calling me right now?* **Mobile-Cait-Accept. Press Speaker.**

"Hey did I wake you up?" She sounds concerned yet enthusiastic.

"Not really, kind of... what's up?"

"What are you doing?"

"You're on speaker by the way... Uh, I'm just so tired. Had to deal with shit today. Probably going to get written up for the second time. New guy messed up, and I took the blame for it."

"The hell happened?"

"I was the leader and he back flipped, smashing this, uh..." I scratch my head and let my hand slide down my neck, "... kid in the foam pit."

"Whaaat!?"

"Long-time friend, rough childhood. They would've fired his ass if they found out it was him—I referred him too. The parents went all stupid about it."

"I didn't even know you got your first write up."

"A couple of weeks after I got hired, I didn't wake up for a shift. Had a million missed calls."

"Wow, that's shitty."

"Yeah."

"Got it—well... You should come to Hollywood with us! We're celebrating Ayla's birthday." Her voice sets fire all of a sudden.

"What? Haha. Who are you with?"

"The girls from work, plus one of their other friends."

"Hm, something about the girls real-quick. So, No L worked the office at the birthday party this afternoon. We had a mix up with the money and she was freaking out a bit, but I said I'd take care of it. Cecily came back afterwards because she borrowed No L's car. That's when I figured they were best friends."

"*Why do you always call Ayla, No L? It's so confusing.*"

"Oh. A couple of times after we met, I kept calling her Layla, so she says something like this to me: 'to get it stuck in your head, remember this: my name is Ayla. It's like Layla, but with no L.'"

"*That's funny. Does she know that?*"

"I don't think so. But, she's cool. Just silly jokes… anyways…"

"*Yeah, go on.*"

I immediately press my hands on the mouthpiece as I yawn. "So, they told me they had something planned tonight, but they weren't specific."

"*Yeah, you should come with.*"

"Wait. Let me tell you another thing. Last night, I came by and said hi to everyone, right? I saw Cecily and asked if she was hungry, so we decide to go to some café after work, but I didn't give her my number and I didn't have hers then."

"*Damn, son.*"

"So, I didn't know what was going on, cause I was there for thirty minutes waiting. Then around midnight, No L texts me asking about how Cecily and I were supposed to go somewhere. So, I thought three things: either Cecily is texting her right now, or Cecily is there with her, or Cecily, is using her phone to text me. I thought to myself, girls, damn it, I know what's going on." I rub my eyes. "It was real funny."

"*Yup, Cecily is obsessed with…*" She doesn't say you, but I felt it on the top of her tongue. "*Well, come on! Come with us!*"

"I'll think about it. Where are you going now?"

"*Going to get ready at one of their houses not sure which yet.*"

"How long have you girls been getting ready?"

"*Yo, dude! Girls gotta get well and ready.*"

"It's been hours since I saw the two."

"*If it takes hours, then so be it!*"

"Haha, okay."

"*Alright, well…*"

"Well… have someone text me the details—where are you now?"

"*I'm almost there.*"

"Yeah, have someone text, please."

"*Okay, I will—but come! We can finish our dance choreo too! Bye-ie.*"

"Haha! Maybe! Take care." **–End Call**.

As I stand up, I stumble over shoes and binders on the light-deprived carpet floor. A small yellow glow passes through the small crevice underneath the door adjusting my eyes to the dark. I travel to the restroom squinting. *Ding!* I turn the faucet from hot to off, brush my eyebrows with my finger, kill the lights, and eagerly rush towards my room. ***Ding!***

Cecily

Sat, Nov 22, 2014, 7:39 PM

Hey it's Cecily!!

My eyes smile.

Hi, Cecily

I was told to text you about
the plans for tonight

I'm ready to receive

"Ready to receive? Oh, Jesus," I whisper to myself.

So were going to the club.
It opens at 10, but it's in
Hollywood so were gunna
leave here around 930ish.
Were girls so it takes us
longer to get ready haha.
So we can just meet you
and whoever else you're
going with there in line

'Were girls so it takes us
longer to get ready,' she
says. Hahaha
I thought you're already
ready when you visited
work

No no no haha
Far from it

So you're gonna put
more make up on?
(>_<)

Don't judge me haha
You're 20 right?

Yes

And is Cait there already

Yeah she's with us rn
And oh okay jw. Cuz the like
under 21 is $20 cash only

I got Benjamin's for
days, I'll be fine if I
decide to go
Do you have $20 cash?

Haha well fine then
And me? Yeah haha why?

You lied to me this afternoon

Because I knew I needed it
for tonight haha I was saving
it

; /

Sorry :/

What time are you
planning on leaving the
club?

Were leaving around 930

"...Leaving the club"

Wth haha
Idk like around 1
or 2 hha why?

Lol
why? if I come, I need to
know the plan

Meet us there around 10!
Haha

If I go, I will probably
not be going home at 1
or 2. Are you three
going home afterwards?

Yeah same for us. And idk
going back here

I'm not going to assume
I'm   welcome   just
because   I   go   to
Hollywood with you.

Idk it's up to her. But we'll
all be pretty tired. So you
should meet us there and
then hangout with us there
and then leave around the
time we do?

There's a line to get in
this place?

Yes

There's no way in hell I'm
getting there at 10

Why not?

> I'm picking up the highly
> desired goods from the
> friends

Ohh gotcha

> Tell me when you leave

Okay. Were leaving in 5 mins

I review the text messages. *Holy fuck! I'm a fucking dick. No emojis? 'Haha's' aren't there. Benjamin's? Are you trying to fuck yourself? What are we? In middle school being awkward thirteen year olds? Go get dressed rookie, damn.* I shake my head to rid of my cringe before it brings me more shame.

"Alright, should I go?" I whisper under my breath. I jump slightly backwards and crash my body on to the bed. I stretch while letting out a yelping type of groan. "I don't know if I should go-awhhh!" I release my fatigue with forceful fury.

"What?" A voice comes out of nowhere surprising me.

"Miel! Next time knock, please!" My sister's silhouette poses in front of the orange light.

"*Sumisigaw ka!* (You were yelling!)" she exclaims with concern.

"Sorry. I'm just stretching. Go help Yanie with her homework!" Her shadow disappears. I stand and stumble through the darkness again trying to reach the light switch. *Okay, Cait. I'll go. I accept your invitation. And absolutely everything that comes along with it.*

Each letter on the sign flickers on and off. H-O-L-L-Y-W-O-O-D. *Welcome to the Garden of Heathens! The land of the Honest! The District of the Diverse!* Winding through the streets with open windows, I'm thoroughly convinced that it's always a night out for masked wingless angels and demons in suits and dresses. *There's my kind of people.* The decadent scent of club sandwiches, spicy chicken wings, gyros, and the easily recognizable Asian plates tickle my nostrils with familiarity. Hey, you can only use these restrooms if you buy something! the sign says with a slap in the face. The cityscape is almost like an amusement park, except, this might actually be the happiest place on Earth—I take that back. I'm not drunk yet.

I signal to turn right towards an alley that is alienated from lights. I slow down for a speed bump. *Classics Lot, $20 Parking.* "Hey man, can I park here? And get my shit together before I pay?"

"Uh, *is* twenty dollars," he replies with a serious eyebrow raise.

"I'm sorry, I couldn't hear. Can I get my stuff together before I decide to park here?"

"Oh *yah, tha's* fine my friend. Just go there." He points with his half-assed index finger to wherever. I choose the spot placed in a delicious corner, closest to him. *Be safe car while I go be unsafe.* "Tanks buddy. Just exit out *tha* way later." He shines his flashlight on the fences barricading a church of beige left shadowed by night time.

"Appreciate it," I reply back.

I stroll through the fumes rising from the sewers, and the fabric-soft steam from the laundry facility dispersing in the air. Everything is somewhat silent. The edges of the street-signs and buildings are all straight. *God and I know, they won't be for long.*

Circles, rectangles, triangles, squares. Green, yellow, red, blue, purple, orange. I turn left towards an electronics store with an ATM. I go in.

"It costs *fifty* dollars to take money out from this machine?" I repeat what the slender pimply Asian guy softly uttered.

"Uh, yeah," he answers. He reveals his crooked yellow teeth inside a smile, brighter than a mannequin's ass-cheeks behind the blurred windows in the whore store next door.

"Damn, alright. Thank you." I leave immediately.

Down the streets and the side streets and the side of the side streets, I cross with a myriad of people. *More circles, rectangles, triangles, squares. Green, yellow, red, blue, purple, orange. Hm. The girls better look damn good because it's hard to beat four of a kind queens with a jack of clubs as a high card. Haha, of course they will. They always do.* I giggle at my thoughts as a couple strolls pass me with their regalia alongside a whirlpool of tatted fellows. The guy almost matches my maroon suit and night-time dress shoes.

"This one goes out to Rachel!" Jesus screams at the crowd into a muffled mic. He's the main attraction in the face of Hollywood and Highland tonight. I don't need to stand with the audience of mixed-feelings to hear. I turn left towards the theater. An Asian tour of what could be a hundred-people made a train all the way from the second floor of the complex to the hallway's entrance. What I really looked into was their weapon of choice, the camera. It's so efficient in keeping treasured moments in captivity. They throw their flash on, even when it's not needed, and by using their lenses as scopes, they shoot these running memories. After the *click*, the tourists all rejoice at their smiling trophies, caged inside colored pixels. *Pictures could be the most sacred of all real things.* They might have been lost though because many of the stores are already closed, but I don't know. I walk on forward. Candies are sweet, coffee feeds energy to the soul, and tables with two chairs sit photographers making love with their photos and students punishing their pens and paper. Or, maybe the other way around.

I climb the great stairs of the complex. My eyes are burning of colors, but I don't mind. Crimson and gold patterned marbles rest at the base of the porcelain white steps. The pillars before the theater are rock strong. *Ring! Ring!* **Mobile-Cecily-Accept.**

"Where are you girls…? I can't hear. Whah?"

"*We're at the third floor in the line—*" **–End Call**. *Service sucks.* I suddenly become conscious of the bouncing airwaves, reverberating back and forth from booming sounds. I go up the staircase, sometimes skipping a step. The terrace serves as a beautiful sight downstairs.

Attached underneath the Asian maroon umbrellas are candy-red and rice-white globe lanterns. Guys and girls sit on wooden bamboo chairs, waiting for their invited friends. Looking at the inside, the ambience and the feeling of red and darker red are so effective with using the Japanese effect to attract the tired and hungry eyes. My stomach protests its emptiness with a pinching gurgle. Finally, I see the girls.

"Hello. Wow, well everyone's matching tonight," I say to Cait, who flashes her black dress with savage grace. *If I said I didn't like it, I'd be lying.*

"I'll be over here, so I'll see you in there," she says to me while pointing at the left side of the bridge. The line stretches from the side corner of the restaurant, strategically funneled in a bridge split into two: under 21 and 21-and-over.

"Hey man, left is the 21 and up line. Come over here," says a not-so-gentle man trying hard to organize everyone.

"Yeah, I should be here in the right." The man continues to rudely direct and command. And just as thoughts continue to slip in my mind, I notice a lady in front of me while the girls are a few backless dresses ahead.

"Hi, hello," I greet first.

"Hello." She smiles at me.

"What's your name?" I hold out my hand to shake hers.

"Alessandra." Her name was a climax for the ears.

"Well, that's nice." She deliciously turns to my sentiment. "Where are you from?" Random chattering drape around the background of her foreign accent.

"I'm from Brazil."

"Oh, I love Brazil!" I exclaim a little too hard.

"Have you been there?" She stares at me, obviously doubting my comment.

"Unfortunately, no, but I've heard all about it from friends who are Brazilian." She blushes in the dark. I didn't see the red permeate through her cheeks, but rather the velvet adjustment of her voice, soft to caress the ears. "And I'm familiar with the carnivorous diet."

"Oh, yes. We love our meat," she replies laughingly. *I never knew that a giggle could have an accent.* After being semi-cuffed and inspected, she waits for me.

"It's a night out of town with the Brazilian college exchange students from CSUN," she ecstatically shares.

"Oh, that's—"

"Let's go inside now!" A lady in black cuts me off and shoos us in.

I let my new friend pay first. I extend my twenty dollars towards the woman, and it instantaneously slips away from my hand. *Is this a metaphor for what's going to happen tonight? Only forty dollars to use now.* After paying, Alessandra vanishes in the black curtains of shade and more shade. *Damn. Disappearance. You seemed cool, Miss. I hope otherwise, but I don't think I will ever see you again.*

I smile as I feel a sentimental reminder from inside my wallet. I look up and the girls are posing themselves with their high heels, standing alongside a photo booth. *There are hundreds of thirsty boys and girls in here about to be anointed with the unholy water of the Club God.* I squint and yawn again, attempting to breathe in the mood and the ambience.

"Hello girls!" I sneak up behind Cecily and quickly brush my hands against her hips to softly hint my existence. *These hips won't be available for long.* She turns around with her girlfriends. The monarch orange hair is smooth; fingers didn't measure, eyes assumed. A hug from Cecily is a quick feel of the black dress's strong fit.

"Hey! How are you?" Cecily asks. She smiles with bright, puffy cheeks.

"The drive was alright. Hi Ayla. Happy birthday!"

"Hi! Thanks!" She turns her shoulder towards my chest as I hug her.

"Time to not think of work. Oh…" A girl with raven brunette hair spins around. "… hello. Who's your friend?" Cecily doesn't respond. She's looking at the dance floor, ready. "Hi, nice to meet you," I greet the stranger first.

"Hi! My name's Annette."

"Nice to meet you Annette. My name is—"

"His name is Mark," Cecily unexpectedly interrupts. *Sure, why the hell not?* "Just kidding. That's his pet name."

"Oh, haha!" Annette laughs. I can only see Cecily's left profile, but that grin—I could feel that grin even if my eyes burst into air.

Boom.

Boom.

BOOM.

I leave the ladies to breathe outside. Boys are already lined up to spit their game to girls they had in mind before coming here. *Superficial or natural? I don't know. But be careful of getting sucked inside each other's dick and pussy rotations; that's easier than breathing fresh air in this place.*

I make my way towards the right side of the club where couches are everywhere. The girls flirt and the boys flirt, behind or on top of one another. Every area is covered with this number of people, all decorated with the same clothes. Their makeup kits and cash filled purses are tucked beside their laps, along the small pockets of what was once neat and tidy sofas. The round tables carry the nectar of amplified love and angst that fills each silicate glass. A man's experienced index finger swirls around the rim of the glass, plunging itself into a horny dip. The wet finger is now up and around a girl's purple shaded lips. With a glare of intentionality, her lips then shut, keeping the finger a prisoner of the tongue. He slides it out. *Smooth.* I stare once again at the glass filled with the same liquid now circulating the girl's mouth. I rush for the outside to avoid any anxious beating of my heart.

I stand close to the ledge of the patio, absorbing and internalizing how the speakers aren't as loud out here. Cars and street performers are still up and running. People are still crossing the streets and the side streets and the sides of the side streets. The world can't seem to stop itself. I stand, wait, and contemplate, eating all the time away. I would sit and relax and touch the couches gowned with periwinkle sheer curtains held by steel drapery, but instead I opt to go back inside the dome of fuckery. I lean on a tall, slim table next to the main entrance. Now, I wait and watch.

Two, three, four, five. Imagine a litter of boy puppies all freshed out with some elevated Nike's and dance tight jeans, cool leather and funky gel held hair, all lined up to receive the number of them hot girls with A+ tits proportional to their skinnier than a guitar neck torsos, giving the pups the juicy non-committal milky kisses, who count nightly victories with how much skin they've gotten to touch from the flirtatious squeeze they managed to achieve in a max of thirty seconds before the girls' interest goes away.

"There she is!" Cait throws her hands up and activates the killer eyes.

"Yeah, boy!" The informal hug is given. She and I walk towards the group. Boys are still hanging out, falling slowly inside a little pit located at the tip of their penis. The two girls hold the front line while No L presses her generously proportioned self on the cold metal walls of the photo booth. Numbers are exchanged. Sex hints are passed from one hip nudge to another. There's no shame—only licentious grace.

"Alright guys, off please. Saying hi to my—"

"Caitirina!" Cecily greets Cait loudly.

"Cecilia! Ayliana!" The black-dressed ladies huddle shoulder to shoulder.

"Would you take a picture of us?" Cecily asks me excitedly. I take it. *The pic's alright. The lighting here sucks.*

"Ew, I look gross! Not posting that!" I feel her delete the picture. "Let's go to the dance floor now!" And here I am, feeling like a dead weight of the group dynamic and I'm not quite sure why.

I've got a red suit on, god damn it. And even if I turn into a hard metal with no other elements to mix with the natural chemicals in my brain, I'm still going to be a man of steel chained, shackled to these black dressed Lois Lanes—didn't anticipate that the fucking club is this well-dressed ghoul's crypt tonight.

"Why do you look all down?" Cait asks me.

"Let's get out of here and go to the bar for some drinks." Cait moves without question. The two girls are on their toes while No L is idle behind their swaying hips. Cait and I advance towards the bar. Traveling towards the fountain of youth requires wiggling around the horde of steel-cologne gents and armor shining ladies. "Alright Cait, what are you gonna get?"

"Straight whiskey. No chaser," she says firmly.

"How much is that?"

"I don't know, I'll tell you in a sec."

"Just save me Cait—save me," I whisper to make sure she can't hear. And so, the second that she takes speaking to the bartender is the first grand pause of this raging night.

In the beginning, there was no sound or light; only stage operators in black, setting up the gig to come. Then, next came the thump. THUMP, THUMP, THUMP. Out of the cluster of nothingness, the first motion let itself be known. BOOM. Indispensable! Irreplaceable! This is modernity's unmoved mover, the groundwork of all bodily sensation, the feet of each tremolo, the father of each mid, the eater of each fade, the life of each live performance—the mother-fucking bass. The pounding of this basic motion travels through matter in every taken space all throughout the complex, even to the empty tundra of a parking lot. It warps the senses and brings about indescribable feelings until you realize that the black images that stand next to you, purchasing drinks, or hitting on chicks, or shaded figures furthering their black form with black dresses, are all happy... but there's the enemy.

Wait... what enemy? What culprit with a knife—? It's the fucking outside world, left unaffected by the bass. They know it's there. They know its magical properties. But they are left unconvinced... Why do we dance? Why do we sing? Why do we hold each other's hips? It's because the bass is a blanket of comfort wrapped in curious eyes and disobedient feet. Hands shackled high and ass pushed low, arms waving like maxed out windshield wipers.

Ah! All that the bass does are great wonders: parting the sweaty sea of fuck boys and girls, turning water into hard alcohol ready for consumption, healing the spirit of the blind by assuring that they can still feel the bounce of the ass-cheeks left and right, and feeding the glutinous poor by demanding for them to spend more of their soul by making it rain with invisible money—doesn't, matter. I may have had too many drinks at this point that I now roam the crowd, bumping into shoulders of those whom I don't even know. I said things I shouldn't have said. Or maybe I should have. I spoke either truth or lies, or some other words that meant nothing. Or maybe they meant everything. I could hear nothing but this calling to join in this youthful recklessness. Cecily, Annette, No L, and Cait are having their way, and as long they're safe and enjoying themselves, I'm having mine. I think.

Help me enjoy. Bless me with your undying ferocity and humble destruction. Let me assume the degenerate role. I can feel awesome powers slapping each corpuscle in my body, ah—! A corpuscle is a biological term for a moving, living cell, like a white or red or black or Asian cell—not gonna be a cell-ist, although no matter what they say, all cells are not created equal. So, that is why I'm about to take form as the cerebral-cellular commander. Give me a few more drinks Cait. Send them, funnel them, creep them my way... I'm here. And I'm ready to receive. Club God waits for the coming of...

I look at my phone. *Three hundred and ten messages?* "You've got to be kidding me?" *The group chat with the guys is out of control!* I try hard to read, but I pocket my phone instead.

The suit is off. The only thing in between the humid air and my inflamed skin is a tight black button up. The bathroom is twenty paces in front of me. *But who's counting? I didn't.* I turn right to go in.

"What's up man?" A black gentleman welcomes me.

"Hey, what's your name?"

"Sif, my man."

"Cool, nice to meet you Sif." He's a bigger guy, wearing a burgundy button up with white dots and stripes, and dreadlocks tucked underneath a fedora. *That's definitely still a thing, I love it.* The stall is to my right, wet underneath. *What the fuck are you looking at?* My tile reflection is staring at me all funny like. *Get your shit together. Too strong out there! Too strong!* I borrow one of the colognes in the sink before I leave the piss and sin stained bathroom.

11:11 PM. *I'm so pumped I wished I wasn't so tired. Damn, I also wish No L isn't on the couch during her birthday celebration, but she is.* "What's going on here?" She doesn't answer. I tap her right leg. "You okay?"

"My stomach hurts." Her face crunches towards the middle. I stare at her and wait for a minute.

"Okay. Feel better!" I leave and arrive at the crowd. Hips are now unavailable, just like the prophecy foretold. Above the temple, hip-held girls and boys are invited to get low. DJ Kane mercilessly shafts the audience from the head of the stage where circles spin when scratched and volume is increased above the maximum decibel limit.

"Hey man, check out these moves!" This Aladdin-look-a-like is here to get on the cat-daddy grind joining in our flow.

"Are you serious?" My body is straight. I stop to a dance break.

The second grand pause of the night hits me in the balls with oscillating pitches. Blow us up DJ. Equip me with all of your troubling tremolo and trembling tenor.

"You know what this means?" I ask him dead in the eye. "It's a dance battle!"

"Yeah? Oh, shit! Everyone back up!" He hollers with extreme vigor. The dance circle widens, getting hot with the friction of each foot back pedaling. *Dash your recipe inside the wok of fame! Snap. Snap... snap. Five, six, five, six, seven, eight.* DJ Kane is counting the meter in rhythm for my poetic motions. One circulation of a violent windmill is enough for the transition to hammered head spins—in the fifth rotation now. The body is absorbing the audience's fury. Pulsing nerves, gutsy creativity, and memory of hours upon hours of falling join in to hoist my fallen legs to a heated side freeze. *Bam! Hit the beat!* Elbow stabbed on the lower abdomen. *Hold. Hold! That's a set.*

I stand straight, staring at the prince of Persia's dance space. "Where my b-boys and b-girls at?!" The girls are excited, all riled up. The guys take the space that's been sweat on by a wasted dancer. "Where did my suit go? Oh, yes— Cecily, thank you."

"Oh, my god! That's the dancer we know! We got a video of that!" Everyone starts dancing again. *Opportunity for anything strikes at 12 AM to a new day.*

"What is this?!" The music ends without a last breath. Arms dangle down. Everyone aimlessly turn their heads at each other. There's a spotlight on the stage above the couches seating countless feet that almost tripped me earlier in the night. We don't even know it, but we're in the front row. Looking up from DJ's set-up, the performance stage is to the left. Three girls emerge in triangular formation, each one holding on to a microphone.

"Alright. Okay. Let's check this out," someone says from behind me.

"I… crazy love… let's do… and…" The mics are crap but at least the beat is sweet enough to taste.

"Hey!" says Aladdin. "Something's wrong."

"Fuck yeah, something's wrong!" I tell him while keeping still from the drunkenness.

"They need back up dancers!" I can see his head blow steam.

"Fuck yeah they need back up dancers!" I reply with fire in my head.

"Let's go!" he says wildly.

"Let's go then!" There's no unstopping my first step forward.

"What the hell!?!"

"No way? Really?"

"Mark, what are you doing? This is crazy!"

"You girls keep yelling questions, and keep making up names, and I seriously don't know why." Aladdin and I jump onto the couches which feel featherlike; each step is a slight tingle of pillow lust. We enter the show on the edge of stage right. Our feet stumble to catch the choreography's beat, but the girl directly to my front holds her mic tight and sends a smile towards my way— that makes me real-happy.

But as usual, the *outside* always loves ruining the fun. A security guard charges from the left as he yells for Aladdin and I to leave. My foot deepens the cushions from jumping off of the stage. I disappear in the crowd. Proud eyes stare at me. "Oh, my god, Mark! What the hell was that?" Cecily passes me my jacket. I slip it on. I don't hesitate to take Cecily's wrist to snatch her phone. Her lips and eyebrows decline to a scowl and a frown.

"I don't approve of the video. Erase it! Please," I yell at her.

"Hey! Hey! You're hurting me." I surrender the phone and leave the scene. My shoulder is slouched, dragged by fatigue, and now a sudden and overwhelming sense of brief guilt. *You're a piece of shit!* My reflection on the tile is staring at me all funny, again. I bit my lip and I commit to not looking at it. Sif's to my right dusting off his extra-extra-large button up.

"Sif, you've been here for hours man. How do you do it?"

"By standing man. Just stand up!"

"These girls man. I'm telling you—something else." I shake my head.

"Yeah. Have fun! You want some bubblegum? Only sixty-five cents!"

"Sure, why the hell not?" The coins stuck in my wallet will finally be put to good use. My reflection flips me off before I leave.

I don't know where the girls are, but I know No L's still on the couch. "Does your stomach still feel bad?"

"Yes…" I hear nothing else after she affirms. My body sways a little towards the left; our shoulders may or may not be touching. I get up and decide to look for the other girls. At the heart of the stage, they stand all crane-like, with skin as smooth and white as fresh Egyptian papyrus, but with sharp and sexy talons clenched above the stage floor. Cecily stands in front of me. *Fuck. The little boy's starting to like her. If you're not careful, I'm going to laugh at you again when you see my face in the bathroom. Don't be stupid!*

"Cecily, I want to show you something… is that cool? It'll be a second." *Oh fuck! No, no, no, no!*

"Sure! What is it?" Cait and Annette examine us.

"I want to show you what I wrote about you." *Oh… Too late… You… fucked up.* I lead her through the crowd, not able to distinguish whether I'm holding her wrist or my dick like a ten-year-old degenerate. It's a cruel thing. *I wish, she can read my mind.*

The world stands still with us in front of the couches. The scent of cigarettes howl against the amalgam of perfumes and colognes in this parched air. She looks like she's listening, but she's giddy. Her head fidgets, she keeps biting her fingers, yet she is still managing to smile well—less like a queen, and more like a princess who has so many wishes, but to the discontent of her heart, there's never enough stars.

"Do you want to go back in?" I ask. She keeps fidgeting.

"Yeah! Can we, uh, talk about this outside later?"

"Yeah, that's fine with me." *Not!* She leaves. I stop a random guy to speak to him about how I feel. He's listening, I think. So long as it looks like it, fake or not, I just want to be at peace.

She now has control over you. Making you feel this way. This fantasy, this dream, what a character in a story of traps and power! Run before these girls cuff your horns, ripping it from your big head and eat it for their late-night snack... let me in your eyes! Then afterwards, let me in everything else—stupid. Why haven't you learned yet, you piece of shit? Look at you smiling like a little punk.

I breathe out and the moist covers my reflection on the tile. The voice is still fucking my ears. *You one of those sissy wusses, fragile as fuck? The fuck are you doing? Man, everyone's asleep, just, go...*

"You alright man?" I ask Sif.

"Always up and ready to go my brother." He's never moved from his spot. I tip him the rest of the cash I have. I have zero dollars left. "The men's bathroom is a club man's best friend. Come again!" Important words for me.

Water is all I can afford. The cup costs a dollar and with great luck, there's four quarters in my suit's inside pocket. I speak to this girl across the counter. There are no chairs. I stand, she stands.

"Hi. My name is, uh, Nathaniel." *What a stupid lie.*

"Tonya. Pleasure." She smiles with a sly I-need-to-get-back-to-work look. But before I leave, she asks, "So, what do you do?"

"I'm a millionaire looking to write more stories about my luxurious and crazy ass life."

"Oh, uh huh." She forces a giggle.

"Can I get a refill, please?"

"That's another dollar." I press my face on the cold surface of the booth. She laughs and says, "I'll take care of it."

"Thank you so much. I appreciate it a lot."

"Take care tonight Mr. Millionaire," she tells me with the same grin I've received from every other girl in this tired and weary place.

"You too." I wish I could tip her something, but my soul just has enough to take me home. I visit my reflection, well really to take a piss.

"Thank you for everything tonight brother."

"Hey, hang in there man! All you gotta do is stay up. You cool and smooth. Nice suit too," Sif says to me.

"Peace," I call behind as I exit. *I don't think I will ever see him again.* I lean against the wall outside the bathroom. I wait to see if I can spot the girls, but I think they disappeared too quickly. The only magic left is in the flickering of lights. But that's not even magic really because I know how it works. The sea is now a lake of girls and boys ending their evening with one last dying dance. They overflow into a river of sweat. The stream leads to the red neon sign that whispers to the eye, "exit." So, I swim to it.

I'm *outside*. Voicemail greets me when I attempt to call the girls. I stand and wait, tired and sleepy, with boyish patience next to chairs and tables of the closed shut-to-the-world restaurants. And slowly, I can feel a voice pushing itself out of my ears only a few moments ago, now slithering inward towards my quickly saddening eyes.

>*You can check downstairs to see if they're waiting for you.*

Stop! I'm going to see the girls and tell them...

>*You're going to be honest? Can't wait. You started writing a little thing about this girl then fell in love with what you wrote. You a stupid fuck! You fucked up tonight and you're gonna want to fix it. You're gonna want to fix it, like you always do. And if you really try to fix this, the way that you always think will solve everything, that'll be it. When you destroy yourself, I'll be here to borrow your eyes, to witness. God and I can't wait...*

I suppose, until then, you'll just have to go away for now.

"Sir, please exit out that way. We're closing the whole place down." I don't acknowledge the man telling me to leave; I subconsciously show myself out. *There are people downstairs waiting for me, or looking for me too—they have to.* But this alcohol is holding me up, while friends support their friends as they all walk down the dead escalators. *I had fun girls, thanks. But you're not even at the underground lots while here I am getting closer and closer to hell.* I climb up the complex; there's nothing for me down below. Jesus is no longer where he was singing. Five more steps and then I'm back in the side of the side streets. *Fifth step, fourth step, third step, second step, one left.*

The third grand pause of the evening is certainly an indefinite last. I feel the whole night rewind in a second as the past follows me from behind. This pause is as simple as the declining black, so easy to know. It's so comfortable—this tiny decrescendo, a speck of a collapsed Hollywood star, this brief black hole in time. The bass devours the fade slowly to its last gulp of the night before it also disappears within itself; I let it take me under. So, I fade under the shadow of the mall's back. I fade into the corner of the janitor's cleaning supply closet. I fade inside of the ATM's deposit dispensary. I fade into the charcoal lines dividing the white tiles. I fade into the grand pause itself. I fade to the streets of tomorrow morning.

I'm still looking for a restroom to piss in. I stumble upon a closing theater and a man with a big belly and overlapping chins tells me to leave. I cross the road, looking left and right at the last lights flickering on and off. The restaurant with the random combinations of Asian, Mexican, and Greek food on its highlighted menu is still open. *Oh! Thank you, Lord, it has a bathroom.*

"I'll honor your sign, but can I, can I use the restroom first?" The Greek lady nods with piercing eyes and the cook to her right stares at me with a vacant expression. I enter the restroom. My phone is set on the top surface of the urinal unlocked. **1:48 AM**, **November 23**, it says. I relieve myself the tingling feelings of piss tickling my jaw and legs. I wash my hands and wipe my fingers. As I exit out, I feel like I missed something. Scavenging through my pockets, I find another dollar instead of my phone. I go into the bathroom and it sits there alone on top of piss. After contemplating a quick dash, I purchase some random chips for 99¢. I open the front door after saying my thanks. **Mobile-Cait-Call.** *Ring! Ring!*

"What's going on? I've been calling!" I am unnecessarily frustrated.

"Where are you?"

"No, where are you? I don't know where I am."

"I'm laying down at one of the girls' houses, I forgot which one. I'm so tired!" I turn left towards the alley with lines that are too straight. God and I know, they're still too straight.

"I've been walking Sunset for two hours now." Establishments that once *boomed* and *clapped* are now in deep sleep.

"What the hell are you doing?"

"Was looking for a restroom." I hold my breath because the fabric-soft steam, which was once dispersed in the air, is not here to save me from the strong scent of the fumes rising from the sewer. "… Wait a second."

"I have to be quiet, the girls are sleeping."

"What? It's only been forty-five minutes, and you're already home? What time did you girls leave?" The guy taking care of my car has already gone home.

"I'm just messing. We're still driving. We're around Westlake or something. I'm still so up there, so drunk!"

"Damn it, Cait." She laughs. I stand and embrace my car. "Who's driving?"

"Ayla. She didn't have anything. Wait… What are you saying 'damn' for? We left the club an hour ago. We couldn't find you so we left."

"Alright. That's fine. What about the video you took? Can you erase it?"

"But why?"

"Because…" I look at my non-self that moves with me inside the car window's reflection. My face is pathetic. "… Because, it's not something I agreed to. There's no consent."

"No. We're keeping it."

"Cait, I'm going to be so upset at work on Tuesday."

"*Alright, alright!*"

"Girls…"

"*Everyone's asleep, just go home…*" **–End Call**.

I'm not hungry anymore…

Hahahahaha…! See?! You honest gentleman! You opened the door only for the girls to close it on you… The District of the Diverse. The Land of the Honest. Come back to the Garden of Heathens. Each letter on the sign is off. H-O-L-L-Y-W-O-O-D. The girls walked their clubbed dog tonight. Hahaha, ha-hah…

Mobile-Gigs-Call. *Ring! Ring! Ring!*

"Hey! Are you awake?" *Damn, I want to hang up right now.*

"*Yeah, man. What's going on?*"

"I called Daniel first, but he didn't answer. Then I thought, Gigs it is. Also my bad if you can't hear me. You're connected to the car. Not touching that phone."

"*It's cool. Heh, what's up?*"

"You sound relaxed as... shit man, did I wake you up?" *Slight shame knows its way around me.*

"*Yeah, but it's chill. I'm gonna get me a glass of ice water.*"

"You want to go back to sleep?"

"*Nah, it's cool. I'm up now, kinda, for a lil' bit.*"

"Alright, well, where do I begin?"

"*Sup?*"

"So, today, I was at work, did a birthday party at the gymnastics place as a leader. Kids were cool. Parents were fine, until my understudy back flipped on a kid. Definitely some stupid shit."

"*Yeah, alright.*"

"Wait up... I'm thrown off. I think this is the most mellow we've been the past ten years."

"*Uh, haha. Yup.*"

"Alright so, I pass out dead. That was two to five in the afternoon. I wake up at seven-thirty from a bunch of texts from people I said I'd hang out with before I passed out. Then, I, uh, got an invite to go to Hollywood and so I said, 'eh, alright, I'll go Cait—oh, that's right... you don't know. Cait's one of the girls."

"*Uh huh...*"

"So, I did. Went to Hollywood. Parked at this lot that cost me twenty bucks. Met up with three other girls. And the club itself was twenty bucks. So, got hammered, things were cool, did some breaking, and we actually got a circle going. It was—it was, pretty nuts. But then..."

"*Wait. What's breaking?*"

"Ugh. Haha. Breakdancing."

"*Ah.*"

"But listen. I took one of the girls outside the patio and said, like a nice middle school kid, 'I wrote something about you,' and she seemed not interested cause she was shaking, looking like she wanted to go back in... dude I was such a fuck. After she went back in, I stood there *cussing* myself out. Met this guy who I spoke to about the whole thing for three minutes, and he said something like, 'hang in there' or something like that."

"*Yeah, I feel. I feel.*"

"I keep remembering all of these things that happened, all blurs at the time—... oh my god..."

"*What?*"

"I think I called one of the girls a slut."

"*Dude... I don't like that...*" There is pain hearing his disappointment.

"I cussed myself out in the bathroom for it. Holy shit... I didn't remember doing that until now. What the fuck!"

"*That shit's wrong man... so, what happened after?*"

"I was walking around Highland and Hollywood looking for a restroom for like, two hours... my body took care of itself, and it was weird. It just knew it had to drink lots of water and piss."

"*... Are you still buzzed?*" His concern is honest.

"That's why I called—so someone can keep me up. It's been awhile since you moved to Sylmar too. Just wanted to laugh things off tonight."

"*Yeah.*"

"I thought you'd be up, maybe doing more than just drinking ice water."

"*There's no girl tonight, if that's what you mean.*"

"Well that's one of the things I meant."

"*Yeah... anyway. Just chilling out man.*"

"The thing is, they're also co-workers. Definitely gonna be seeing them real soon. The feels are like middle school all over again, damn."

"*Did you, uh, call Gabi...?*"

"She didn't pick up. I'm thinking of going to visit her."

"*Alright... you should go do that. And be careful.*"

"Yeah, I'm careful."

"*Where are you?*"

"The 101—just passed Van Nuys."

"*Alright, well, Imma go back to sleep.*"

"Thanks a lot for talking. We'll chill sometime. Hit me up."

"*Yeah, that'd be chill—and, yeah. Go and talk to her.*"

"I should, huh?"

"*Yeah...*"

"Alright. Thanks a lot." *You're right, but I'm scared about telling her.*

"*Take it easy, peace,*" he tells me in the softest way I've ever heard him speak.

"Peace..." I mumble back. **–End Call**.

There's an orange warning sign flickering on and off. SLOW DOWN. I blink rapidly because my right eye contact has a speck swimming above my cornea, irritating it to tears. I exit the freeway on De Soto. A red light above grey trees meets me on each intersection. I write notes on my phone as I hit each stop. Parallel parking buzzed has never been so easy. *Damn, I could have killed someone...*

Sigh. This light post above was made for me. The city made it for this moment. They knew I was going to be here.

Cait
Sun, Nov 23, 2014, 2:46 AM
I need to talk to you

I take off my suit jacket to cover my skin infested with goose bumps. ***Ding!***

Are you ok

You want to read some I wrote just now... I don't know if I told you but I've been writing a lot

What is it? go ahead

Whenever you see that person who looks at you and gives you that eye, don't look back. It's only a glance. It's a promise that is left said with empty words, or should I say empty eyes. I'm an author. My name, well wouldn't it be nice to not know; at least, for now. She smiled at me. They smiled at me. The author who has a way with words. The author that everyone claps their hands to. I'm the one! But, I have a prologue that I wrote. I wrote it a week ago. Now, they want to see it, know what it is. They don't ask for it though. But, it's inside their head. They tell you their names, they tell you their songs, you try to sing them, but no one tells you how they really go. I drove 30 miles from nowhere to here.

I appreciate the time. I appreciate the fantasy. I appreciate the ice-cold drinks and the speck of dignity I found on the sticky floor. I appreciate you. Even though you don't know me. But I know your

name. That's all, that's all my dreams
need to know.

If she asked me if I was thinking about
her, I'd lie.

WhTz this about? Wow
That's deep

> Lol that's me
> bullshitting. I was
> driving when I wrote
> that.
> There's actually one
> piece that I really wrote.
> I want to show it to
> someone. Would you
> promise not to tell? Or,
> at least, don't let me
> find out what you told. I
> know I'm being abrasive
> but this shits real. It's
> been real.

Ok drake. Rap it to me

> This is the prologue to
> my book. This is very
> special to me and
> anyone I shared this to,
> I give a shit about

I read it again as she reads it for the first time.

November 14, 2014 11:34 pm

It was November 15, 2014 1:39 am and I
was there writing one of the most
important pieces of my entire life—but at
the time, I didn't know it yet:
I met a girl a few weeks ago, and I didn't
pay much attention to her then. I didn't
think much of her and I didn't find
anything about it so random; not until
something weird happened. Images of her
monarch orange hair, her eyes that smile
with the light of dawn and her soft and
whispery way of saying "that's so sad",
scatter across the edges of my brain,
falling one by one into my little pit of
a heart.

"Damn what a boyish thing to write in paper! And why you gotta lie about the date? November fourteen still got you choked-up bitch?"

But there are things I think about like, sometimes, I think about whether she thinks about me. Cause to me, She's a track star sprinting around my ear, my lips, my nose, my hair, for fuckin' everywhere. When she's tired, she sits and rests inside my eyes. That's where she is and she's tiring me out, cause I have to look at her. I have to. It would be an injustice to not appreciate.

Wouldn't it?

Something is telling me to go, to be, to know this, this somewhere—this *some-here*. She looks at me, like she likes me. I would hate to believe that all of her eyes are pretty lies; *there is,* a chance of that.

I understand that this is the time to please ourselves: to flirt, to dance, to spin, to do a lot of many things! It really is! So come with me! Let's do it! But before that, I'll tell you something I think is pretty. It might make someone throw up unicorns and rainbows, but this girl I've been talking about. She's real. Her name is real also. One thing you can be so sure of is that a woman never lies about her name. Her name is everything and everything is real. She's so real that she makes you think of her realness.

I don't think I'll be marrying this girl. I don't think she's the one I'll be holding hands with tonight. I don't think I'm 'in like' with her... I think.

But me, no matter how much I try, I can't get this reality, out of my thought-releasing, abstract-writing, concrete-falling mind.

If you ever share this.
Share it appropriately.
That's all I ask for.

Oh ok. I won't share it
Hold on drunk and half asleep
You wrote that about Cecily.
Dude that's nuts I'm so in shock

Why so shocking

Because I didn't know you
know her like that. You totally
played it off like you weren't
interested in her at all.
You should've told me you
liked her like that!

Give me an award for
best actor
JK. I'm just an author
writing whilst not sober

You had me fooled wtf!
I thought you just met her
like recently.

I don't know her. The
first
piece was for her

"I mean it was inspired by her... Eh, fuck it."

It just threw me off it's really
well written but I was just
shocked.

I don't kno who she is
But what you read is
what she's done to me

Oh ok I get it now

I think honesty would
destroy everything
As it always does

It's all good, you gotta say
what you feel. You shouldn't
feel that way I try honestly
always say exactly what I'm
thinking it makes thing the
eSiestb
Easiest*

I agree... But not with
girls
Not with girls and me

Lol it's opposite

I've learned
My honesty is too much
Girls can't tell guys what
they're feeling because
guys are capable of
comprehending how to feel
that way back why
Yet* not why

"Fuck that. Most hurt cause they tell all of the fucking time."

It's too powerful and full
of passion that it's so
hard
Yeah you're just different
I don't thnk im too far
off any normal guy.
That's the thing. Sooo
many guys feel. But
were too much of a
puss to own up to it.
I don't want to be an
only-surface friend. I
want meaningful
friendships. That's all.

I just want to give my friends the world. God, is that not okay with you?

Anyways...I wrote that
when I was high and I
was home and I'm like
fuck...What is this
An autobiography or what?
I don't know. Some
creative non-fiction shit
but maybe biography-
like. I just write.
See the thing is I truly
don't know how I feel
And I'm not one to
share my feelings
And I'm not one to talk
to people about how I
feel
Not anymore. At least
I think this is a very
special occasion

You gotta let it out

Lol, I was about to

Yeah I like that stuff

But she said, when we get outside. We'll talk But like I said...instead I went in the bathroom to cuss myself out

If ur gonna write this maybe use different names so no one can tell

Names? Nah, her name stays Everyone's name stays Bc, one day she'll know, one way or another I can't let anything like this left quiet anymore... It's just...There's always a right time. even If characters in my stories have to say it, then they will. Don't worry sharing this with the girls. Before I say anything. I've accepted someone to say it to someone else. Don't delete the video. I hope you didn't. I might regret it tomorrow

Delivered

Outside is the quietest it's ever been. Even during the ride from the city lights to here, there's only been the moon chilling up there, pulling and tugging seas and oceans. These flickering light posts explode into a horizon of a million tightly packed flakes of myrrh and frankincense. *Where do I even start to collect, and gather? What's going on?* The gates and the doors need the tenant's detectors. There's no way to even knock—maybe if I jump the spiky fence. But surveillance and security will ruin what is still left of the night. Being this drunk, I might as well stab my organs to my own death myself. After reading thirty-seven missed-calls on a bold, bright screen, I give up calling Gabrielle. My eyes are closing, but I fight them. There's no sleep until these words in front of me start making sense.

"You know where to begin. Suspect that all the girls know everything. Cait's loyal to the other girls. Tonight was stupid, hasty and dangerously reckless and everyone's irresponsible with their words."

"I want to know if tonight was real or a fantasy."

"I'm not gonna baby you."

"Yeah. I don't think that's a good idea right now."

"You're not a king, or even a prince. At most, you're maybe a jack of hearts, climbing the stalk too high on the clouds and thinking yourself a giant, when all you did was steal thunder whenever opportunity struck."

"I'm so tired, please, let me sleep."

"You're stupid for even writing that. Shut up. What happened tonight can't happen again. You're trapped inside a kid's night time fable."

"The only lesson anyone should get out of this story is—the party self fucked me."

"It's not the party self. You party all the time. Stop bringing the words you wrote about her into reality, especially the way you've depicted her as this heavenly thing when you didn't even know who she was. If anyone were to read what you wrote, they'd think you're in love with her. And we both know you don't (I don't know what people mean by love).

The past year has been good to you. But it has been good because you kept your mouth shut until you had the right thing to say. And many times, you've had the right things. You introduced yourself and let natural flow take its place. Leave the romantic lyrics and the poetry inside your pen's ink or your pencil's lead or your phone's keyboard. Leave no space on the paper for fantasies. You're now doing well only thinking about it—what's done is done. Fix things. It's time."

"When I got hired, they would tell me what I needed to do, or, what rules they set as the appropriate ways an employee should behave. Signing the papers was recognizing there are rules and manners.

Law and structure are supposed to keep us in order, and keep us focused. I appreciate it and I follow it.

I guess we're back to the start again. The question I've had in my head: should I keep this a fantasy? Leave co-workers as co-workers and nothing more? Is that a universal law I have to follow? Because I can go to sleep soundly, and when I wake up, it could've just been a dream. Or I can leave it and not show care? Clock in and clock out as a man left to not give any shit of what he actually cares for— that's worse, I'd rather lose my job than live the rest of my life haunted by ghosts. What if I could fall into a hole deeper than I am now? But any feeling that comes with that, they will remember. The logic of situations doesn't need fixing. It's always the god damn feelings... the realest of all things that needs repair."

"So, don't. Lions are heavy. No matter how strong, muscle is powerful. This can't be fixed with roaring passions and apologies that appeal to the girls' mercy and sympathy. That's going to make you look like a bitch and it's going to kill you in the end of all of this. The body must be flexible, feet must be quick... You have to sleep. Tomorrow, there's a story to write and a boy to kill"

"I write you out to help me. Keep me sane please! If I don't have you helping, the nightmares will win. I'm falling asleep. Fuck. They're coming! Why does the poet in the pilot's seat always open his eyes when I close mine???"

... zzz ...

Who's not the only what? Who's not the only what?

I open my eyes. My yawn closes them shut, again. Blue metal. A van maneuvering in front of me. Parking. Parallel parking. I look at myself wearing my black pants, the unbuckled belt still hanging from my waist, the skin tight black dress shirt, socks that didn't help keep me warm last night, and my red suit jacket used as my blanket covering only the upper body. **10:43 AM**, **13%**, the phone blatantly shows me. *Cait sent a message?*

Cait
Don't worry sharing this with the girls. Before I say anything. I've accepted someone to say it to someone else. Don't delete the video. I hope you didn't. I might regret it tomorrow

Sun, Nov 23, 2014, 8:03 AM

I still have it!

I roll the window down. "Excuse me, miss. Hi. What was that song?" I ask a copper-skinned female wearing all bright colors.

"Oh. It's *Not the Only One* by Sam Smith." *Oh, how fucking appropriate to kick start the day.* She smiles curiously.

"That's right. Thank you." I smile back.

"Yeah! Sure thing!" She leaves. I let the fresh morning air enter and leave my car, breathing in and out. **Mobile-Gabrielle Pilar-Call.** *Ring! Ring! Ring!*

"Hey! Are you awa—?"

"You have been forwarded to an automatic voice messaging system..."

"Agh!" *Ring! Ring!* **Mobile-Gabrielle Pilar-Accept.**

"Hello?" I answer.

"Hi. What happened? You called so many times..."

"Uh, I came last night, after the whole adventure at Hollywood..."

"What Hollywood adventure?"

"Would you let me in? Please? And, I'll tell you everything." **–End Call.**

She comes out with sinking eyes. She's a thin girl in her pajamas and a white top. "Hey, can we talk outside? It's nice outside." The stairwell's grand acoustic amplifies her yes. "I'll wait in the car."

"Let me change then. Be right there," she replies back. I feel banging on my head as if this apartment door is crushing my skull. It's a little heavier opening it from inside.

"I'm sorry for not texting back last night; I accidentally took a nap after work," I tell her. Flowers everywhere sway with vivid colors. "I think the park was a good idea for a place to talk. It's nice out." After she said yes in the stairwell, she changed her attire into a floral-printed sundress that playfully and purposefully hugs the slight curve of her figure. Her right ear bears an earring of soft feathers of monarch orange—*that color.*

"Stop scratching your eye!" Her suggestion is sweet.

"I threw my contacts off last night. Hold up! Did you eat breakfast?"

"I had cereal." *Her common answer.*

"Haha. Again?"

"I like when my teeth crush the little sugar things, they make crunchy noises. You know I don't spend much on food." Her brunette hair smells like fair cherries mixed with a whiff of honesty. "I had to pay rent and also my ballet classes. You'll never guess how much my dad paid me to take his picture!" I look at her with stinging eyes.

"Wait. Why did you talk to him?"

"Don't worry, I was at my parent's house to get some clothes out and he paid me three hundred dollars just to take his picture."

"Why would you talk to him after the—"

"It's fine. I left right after."

"If he does anything to you again, it'll be more than a 911 call…"

"Can we stop talking about this now… so what happened last night?"

"Okay. We can." After last night, even the sound of a kid yelling eight feet away from me about his ice cream melting under the sun is super gentle. And beneath the sun's shining umbrella, I tell her everything I remembered.

"So, do you want my opinion of this?" I look towards my right. Her jaw drops a tiny bit. Her lips pucker and her tongue stabs the inside of her right cheek, traveling to the left, passing the upper lip. It stops before it hits the right cheek.

"I mean, I understand how you might feel a little…"

"No, it's okay. What do you want me to say about it?" Both of her hands rest neatly on her lap.

"I wanted to say sorry last night. But I don't know." She looks behind us. Her focus is at the father yelling at his kid to get down from the top of the slide. Then, her head turns towards the grass. She doesn't look into my eyes, but I gaze at hers, and I know what those eyes are asking for. "Are you okay?"

"Yeah, I'm okay." She shakes her head. "I'm fine. What did you ask again?"

"Nothing. I was saying how I thought of apologizing last night, but I don't think that's going to fix how they feel. If I apologize, it's just, uh, a recognition that I did something wrong."

"Well, I think it's better to apologize than not. What else is there to do other than apologizing? And do you really expect to fix people's feelings? I don't know. That's so, so hard."

"Ignore it?" I answer fast.

"That would be awkward."

"Yeah, I think ignoring is stupid. Well, weak might be a better word."

"Especially, when you're the one who messed up…" Unlocking her phone, she reveals the time. **11:25 AM**. "What's the name of this girl?" Her hands open, urging me to share.

"Cecily…" The name softly rides the wind. Air rushes through the trees, rustling the leaves that still are clinging to the branches for life and the ones on the ground. They twirl from the grass to the playground's edge, landing into the sand.

"Oh…" Her cheeks flare red under the midday sun. "The one that… you wrote about last Saturday?"

"Yeah," I say with a grunt. A praying mantis eats her male counterpart after mating. A caterpillar sleeps inside its cocoon. I watch it intensely when suddenly a bird snatches the silky enveloped insect. *Bastard's nightmare came true damn.* My brain is wrestling with itself. I cough to expel the phlegm of last night's bullshit. I spit behind my left side. *A mantis and a caterpillar are dead, a boy and a girl are dying, and the entire Cosmos could care less. So, we have to just a little bit more.*

"I think you'll figure it out; don't worry too much." After she releases her last statement, my eyes turn towards the afternoon street. The cars look different under the daylight compared to last night. Maybe not too different, but they have a little something here and there; a certain glare that makes them comfortable to look at. "I… really hope you figure it out. But I think you should apologize. I know that's not your thing, but maybe try it here just this once," she sweetly suggests.

"Yeah, you're right. My head hurts." She gently places her fingers behind my pulsing brain and massages it.

"And didn't you say they're coworkers?"

"Yup. I fucked up real-good."

"What if the company learns about this?"

"Handbook states inappropriate relationships are not tolerated, but I'm not even doing that. You would definitely know." She smirks to the side. "I just did something so dumb and stupid. Work is just gonna be, eh."

"Did you ask your guy friends about this?"

"Not yet, but I have an idea of what they'd say."

"It's okay to say that you don't know what to do."

"Timing has to be on point. I need to see how they're feeling." I take out my phone. **Find C-e-c-i-l-y.**

"Why?" She frowns.

"Because if I can find an option to do something that can work better than just going on my knees, I'll take it. I know there's something better. Something that can still…" I pause to gather my thoughts, "… that is still, you know, respectable." I sigh and shrug. "Even if I lose friends, I need to at least be able to live with myself."

"What would that be?" I type on my phone. She stares directly at it, but I don't acknowledge that I can see her hazel eyes trying to grab details to satisfy her curiosity.

"Don't worry. I'll tell you everything that happens in this story."

"What story?"

"I don't even know." We sigh out a breath full of tension.

"Can we just go elsewhere? Somewhere far away? Take a break?" she asks almost pleadingly. I show her a message.

Cecily

Sun, Nov 23, 2014, 11:44 PM

Hey, how are you girls?

Delivered

"Why did you send that?"

"I can't just run away. I have to fix this first. And I promise, we'll go out."

"Yeah…" She doesn't sound so enthused.

"I need to know what she'd say." She puts her head on my shoulders. "… I know how you feel and I understand, but there's nothing going on here with the girls—just friendships. I guess, it's so hard to know with my style of writing." I try to smile as I draw my hands to emphasize what I was saying. So, she takes the opportunity to cradle her pretty little head onto my rough palm; that's when she begins blushing forever. Her head rolls down to rest nicely on my lap. I look up at the sky and the angels who painted it had never been so clean with their whites and blues. Cumulus clouds are placed evenly along this Sunday morning tapestry above the both of us.

"Stay focused on school, okay?" Her voice is muffled. "I know how important that is to you. You just get distracted so easily!"

"Don't worry. Alright…" *I know she knows it will.*

"Are you okay?" She lifts her head off and asks me, while her arms embrace my sinking shoulders. I take her shoulders and push them lightly to see her lotion-smooth face.

37

"Yeah! It's just a passing thing… like my nightmare again last night…"

"Do you remember it?"

"I have it down, yeah. Was writing while waiting for you. Well at least, from what I remember." I pull the document out from my phone. "Well, here. I'll read to you what I wrote."

Imagine, a store, inside a mall, clothes piled on top of folded ones, some lodged in the corner to hide it from everyone else. It was a beautiful sight, all of these reflections on any shining material that lacks anything else but luster, were adjusted with brightness to the max. Exposure was incredibly high too. Everyone's eyes glow like ethereal orbs. Shadows and black point are shifted to the left of the scale. Everything is so dream-like bright it almost feels like being a baby again.

I was walking around with a girl looking at all these things. She told me she was tired so we sat on a blue round table like the ones schools tend to have everywhere. She doesn't look at me, I don't know why.

"You made a mistake. God damn, you're such a fuck," she said to me. I was surprised and I didn't know what to say

"You're ruining a perfectly good moment," I replied.

"How dare you even say that? You hurting girls. You're hurting me. You're hurting us. Anything with you is never a good moment."

"That's all I remember…" I close the document.

"Wow, what does that mean?"

"They never mean anything." I believe my statement.

"I'm not so sure about that."

I brush off the images now hanging in the back of the closet of my mind. "It'll pass."

"Are you sure?" she asks with slow and connected rhythm.

"They're just nightmares. It's okay." The sky's still blue. The grass still house butterflies. Kids are laughing. Parents are babysitting. Nothing has changed outside. But somewhere, something did change. "Do you want to go get food right now? I'll buy today." She looks at me funny. "Don't worry. I'm okay."

"I'm worried about whether I'll be okay," she whispers to me. "I texted you last night about meeting up…"

"I'm sorry," I whisper back.

"It's okay. I just wanted to give you this." She pulls a necklace around my neck and latches it together above my heart. "My grandma gave it to me."

"I don't know what to say when I get gifts," I chuckle.

"You don't have to say anything. And I know that Emily gave you one too. Now, I can be with you too, wherever you go." My heart stops. And within an instant, her blush disappears in the midst of an orange afternoon.

Mi Flora Hermosa… Your smile to me will always be like a simile… I, just has to be there somewhere.

Mood Swings

This is the End. It's all over. I run through Streets of dark cement, tripping on alcoholic Puddles, stepping on the Beer-stained sidewalk perpetually fizzing under the seemingly endless line of dim streetlights. It's a rainy night of no Color. I run, run, and run. I sit down on the sidewalk to catch my Breath. There are no Stars for me to wish for a Way Out.

A little boy appears. He walks towards me dragging something that I can't see. I hear the Sound of chains rattling. Before he gets close enough for the streetlight to put an image to the sound in my head, he tosses it back to the Dark behind; not so I can't see, but so that he no longer has to carry Anything. His Hands are free to play with whatever he wants. The raindrops peel off his Sins from his cheeks.

"Hi," *I say with a serious face.*

"Do you remember happy-girl-Kristin from track?" *he asks.*

"Kristin from track was such an experience, my god."

"Remember when she was with Isaiah? Remember when you knew it when you were both texting her at the same time in World History sophomore year, and for every ten messages he sent, you sent a paragraph in one message after she asked you a five-word question?"

"Yeah, I remember every single detail."

"Remember how she was your lovely little high school lady friend, until you called her, told her you liked her? And even when she said, 'We'll see...' remember when you still had hope? Grant even told you 'girls just say that' and you still didn't listen... remember when you were so fucking stupid?"

"Why are you so hostile all the time?"

"You don't remember high school? Remember when you were the most hostile and violent mother fucker around—even to your love ones?"

"Why don't we compromise, help each other out?"

"Do you remember Emily from cross country?"

"Yes. But answer my question!"

"Do you remember Emily from choir?"

"Yes! Yes, to both! They're the same person! But that doesn't answer my question! Answer my question little child."

"You think I'm the little child? Hm. Hm. Okay. Then tell Cecily how I feel. After that everything will be better." *He speaks so softly; whispers gentler than the breeze.*

"We are coworkers! The handbook stands. And I can't do that because I don't like her."

"You know what's funny—? You tell yourself that it's my fault that you wrote about Cecily... but you were tired and drunk when you wrote about her. It was you... I know it wasn't me... Nothing? You see? This is why I fuck with you. You take care of Gabrielle and you take care of her damn well. But she's not the only one. There's this little itch in the back of your throat, in the back of your spine, in the back of your very back—listen well and listen good. I just want your attention. You don't give me attention. I just want someone to give me the attention I deserve. You blamed liking and writing this girl on a fucking voice inside your hand. Give me attention—but you don't give. You know what you need to do, but you stop yourself from doing it. Remember when Kristin didn't give you attention? Didn't that hurt? Remember when you murdered Emily's feelings? That didn't hurt you. It hurt me. I don't want to hurt anymore. I don't want to hurt anymore. I'm giving up. Please make it stop. Please make it stop. Please make it as stop. Please, please, please..." I don't know what to say. The rain rages on wanting to kill me, just like the boy does. He lets the rain spew thunder as madness descends on my soul. "Please make it stop. I don't want to hurt anymore. I don't want to hurt anymore. I don't want to hurt anymore." The Clouds clamp themselves up in the Sky, acting as a mortar for the black blanket of God while it covers the Machine Guns above shooting at me with Thoughts in the form of Little Tears. I run for cover, but there are no indoors, or ceilings, or umbrellas that these piercing drops of his Tragedy from his skin can't leisurely pass through. His whisper to me, "... Can the little boy just have what he wants? Fuck the handbook. Can I just tell Cecily how I feel?"

"I don't understand why you're crying! Calm the fuck down! It's not that big of a deal!"

"Please make it stop! Just tell her how you feel! Just, please... I don't want to hurt anymore."

"... I don't want you to hurt either..."

"Kill me! Kill me! Use this and kill me!" He runs over to and hands me a knife. I don't want to, but now I'm holding it tight. He let me sink the blade from the top of his cranium, forcing the sharpened-edge of Death onto his Brain. I'm saddened to see red-liquid on my hands, but all I can enjoy is listening and seeing Pain and Pleasure mix upon each slice of his Mind. His Teeth bites onto his Tongue, rendering Blood to flow from his devil-sanctioned Mouth. I love you he says to me. I know, I say back as I continue on to take each perspective, each sense, each thought from exiting his body as Rain wash over the gooey-matter in front of my wet and guilty feet. Half of his face dangles from his mandible still latched on. He looks at me with caring eyes asking for me to remember them before he falls onto the cold ground. He and I stare at each other so intimately, so lovingly, I can't let go of the moment. He holds onto my hand with the knife stuck in between our interlocked fingers. He loves me so much. All we wanted...

What the…! I look at the wall in front of me. Blinds. Cabinets. Books. Computer. Papers and socks are on the floor. Button ups and suit jackets are stacked on top of the suffocating computer keyboard. I scratch my head and turn from my left side to face the ceiling. I'm now on my back. **7:07 AM**, says the clock with a tick. "Ah, shit. It's Wednesday. Ugh! Alright, let's do this!" I have an end-of-the-semester midterm is at eleven-thirty. I tuck my legs to kick off the blankets. *Hm. I have a feeling that I had a dream… but I don't… I can't… remember…*

The library's automatic doors open with ease. Air-conditioned atmosphere hits my freshly showered skin with coolness. But my eyes strain to stay up. All I can remember is what Charlotte from work had asked me yesterday. I feel it on the tip of my tongue, wanting to be expressed with vivid voice. I'm so distracted. A girl, three feet to my left, sitting at another round table, is talking on her phone while eating cheese chips. I don't see her, but I know she's there crunching and the chattering, reminding me of work. My body is numb and deceiving, stuck lying on the table. Anthony from class is supposed to come to study with me, but his saved seat remains empty. I pull my library-borrowed textbook towards me. And in the margins of International Relations, I write my own memories next to some guy named Dom's hand-writing, who apparently hearts *his* Kat very hard.

> NOVEMBER 23 SUNDAY
> CECILY REPLIED TO MY TEXT. SAID, "WE'RE GOOD. SORRY WAS AT WORK."

I didn't respond.

> NOVEMBER 24 MONDAY.
> I VISITED TO FILE A SUB SHEET. CECILY'S REACTION...

I had parked in my usual spot: next to the tree that was in the foreground of a view of the Ocean Side Mountains, stretching from Malibu's raging sands to the plantation fields of Oxnard, to the footsteps of the Valley's beach canyons. I came from school, dressed all fancy in an academic, classy sort of way. I said hi to our office ladies, Staci and Beckie. They were busy, but they gave time for a smile. I was picking up my check. It didn't take long. What took so god damn long was Cecily's eyes. She followed her sister Kiersten with an athlete's posture. I was sitting on a rotating chair, but I kept it idle. Seeing her was like seeing the glitters blow up and waiting for the shimmering lights. I saw the rockets shoot out from the ground to the sky, velocity was on point, but her eyes didn't look. Nothing. There's so much going on with family matters, school, Gabi, and being so tired all the time that sometimes I forget that there are side notes of life. But in this case, I fear that I would forget the main point of it all. And that this side note is going to take up the whole page...

> TEXTED NO L,. ASKED HOW SHE WAS (AFTER I SAW CECILY, SAME NIGHT)

It's like it's not enough that I didn't intentionally buy VIP tickets to this empty firework show, but also, the only thing No L handed me was a grey Helvetica font, seven-point size, fucking read receipt when she saw my message.

NOVEMBER 25 TUESDAY.
HOW WORK WAS LIKE WITH THE THREE OF THEM:
AYLA FIRST 4:03 pm

The office was tucked to my left with no one, but No L. Her back was turned away from me as she printed out some necessary papers for her own business. Her hand was rested on her designer bag resting on the counter. She didn't speak until I said my "hi." I asked, "How are you?" Her reply was unusually unpleasant. With immediate distaste, she said, "fine." I was taken aback by it because I don't think I had wronged her that night too, unless she was pissed off because of the Cecily issue. I asked again how she was and once again, the reply was, "I'm fine!" She didn't emphasize what she said, but instead, the exclamation that followed after; I felt it as I sat down. I went about my own responsibilities of checking for kids who shouldn't have been in my class because they weren't enrolled, or checked if the records were accurate with kid's attendance. I asked her, objectively, to see how she would react, if I could access the computer. She said I wasn't allowed. My eyebrows went up with all the doubt in the world, since I had been previously encouraged to learn and use it before.

THEN CECILY COMES IN 4:07 pm

Cecily entered in, same way as last night, but this time I stood up to see her with her blue work shirt and tight leggings. I usually stand out of habit when I see a person to greet them, but I knew that refraining from saying anything other than a "hi" was probably the right call. Cecily replied a "hi" too, still without eye contact. I sat back down again, but this time I didn't think of it and ended up sitting in No L's chair, the one to my right. The computer in front of me, the one I wanted access to, wasn't even on. After Cecily handed No L a to-go bag, I could see both of them laugh at the screen. The pen in my hand wasn't working, so I didn't have anything to do, but to sit and look at my attendance sheets. Inside I felt shitty, as I should, but the girls weren't confronting me if there was a problem to confront me about, and that was a big problem. That's also why I don't think I should have just apologized outright. I think something else was going on under the surface. The frame of the monitor screen held all of our reflections: No L lodged on the upper right corner, looking down at her food next to the printer; Cecily, to her left, was texting, and three times she looked at me while doing so. We made eye contact through the screen, and the reflection of my face was occupying the entire left side; even the computer was telling me that I was not in the right about any of this. Maybe? Maybe not? For some unknown reason, they left the room. I hadn't started work, was in about twelve minutes, and I had already gotten my rage on.

I went back to my car to grab my change of clothes. The air was fresh. It was breathable. I liked what was going on outside. It wasn't asphyxiating. The grass swayed with me. The shrubs nodded. The branches were cool, they actually said hi, and seemed to notice my presence. I decided to change in my car. I took off my dress shoes and tossed them at the back seat. Dust flew in the air and landed on the seats themselves. It was time to clean, but looking at my car, I didn't know where to start. Hm, what happened after that? My other coworkers entered the parking lot in caravan-style. I waited for them to settle. A dark grey coupe window was rolled down. A question was asked.

"You change out here?"

"Yes Charlotte, I do!" I assumed she had seen me struggle and frown while I ached to pull off my left shoe, which was tied tightly. I realized now that I had unintentionally put off an annoyed look. She didn't confirm that until we spoke later that night after work. My belt was easy to take off, but my pants were tight. I put my grey cotton shorts on. The girls got out. We all went in.

APPROACHED CAIT AROUND 4:21 pm

I passed the office and the lobby room where the parents either let their kids play or demand for them to sit. After I entered through the doors, my first to fourth steps were on the light sky colored carpet. The rod floor, where kids tumble in a straight line instead of the main floor, felt my fifth to eighth steps. The resi mat was lodged on a space underneath two gymnastic high bars. The bounces and springs from the soft cushion were my ninth to eleventh steps. The twelfth step was met with Cait. Greeting her should've been done even before the first step when we made eye contact, but since I didn't know what the fuck was going on, it didn't matter at this point. She didn't tell me what was going on. I'm trying to remember all these details, but there's not a lot of time so—fast forward. I saw Cecily and Cait speak with their back turned against the wall, twenty feet away. Charlotte was close behind them. Cecily giggled.

CHARLOTTE 4:33 pm
SHE ASKED ME HER SECOND QUESTION OF THE NIGHT.
AND PROBABLY WHAT MADE THIS WHOLE THING EVEN
MORE OF A CLUSTER FUCK: "WHAT'S THIS THING THAT
YOU LIKE CECILY..."

Who was squealing, spreading rumors? I want to know.

TEXTED CAIT AFTER WORK

"Just wait for it to blow over, it'll be fine," she said to me...

I look away from the book. **Ding!** *What the hell? What is this?*

No L

Sun, Nov 23, 2014, 10:00 PM

Hey, how are you feeling after all the shenanigans?

Wed, Nov 26, 2014, 11:20 AM

I don't know what you think Cait would tell me but she didn't say anything to me on Saturday about what happened. I don't appreciate you taking me annoyed and pissed at you out on my friends though. They don't deserve it and frankly it makes you look like a jerk. I have my own opinion of people and make my own decisions on how I perceive people. I am mad at you because you wouldn't leave me alone on saturday and you kept touching me when I clearly told you to stop multiple times. It makes me uncomfortable and I don't appreciate it. So stop giving Cait and Cecily shit when they didn't do anything to you

---

I lock my phone. Bright pixels turn into a faint mirror before my vision. I watch my eyes, full of anger. *What have we all done with the workplace?*

My pen's on fire. "Alright, folks. Finish up your last sentence." I finish three before I hand the professor my test.

"Thank you," I tell him. I turn around from students still erasing mistakes. The air kisses my face after opening the door. *Ding!*

> Reminder: Pick up Yanie, 3:10 PM

"Oh, yes!" Outside of the History and Science building, leaves swirl around people who are walking up and down the main concrete road of the college. I sluggishly walk down the skinny steps of the stair case. I turn left towards the parking lot behind the towering Performing Arts building. The sun's shining brightly on my face. *Ding!* "What is this?"

> **T.O. girl Kristin**
> Wed, Nov 26, 2014, 3:01PM
> Hey does your ex girlfriend
> work at star cafe?
>
>   From the latest things I
>   know of her, yes.
> Haha that's funny, she just
> took my order

"I want to know what's funny about this."

>   How was that? Did she
>   recognize you?
> It was good and she was super
> nice! But no I don't think she
> recognized me and I would've
> said hi but I wasn't positive it
> was her lol
>   Was she smiling? Did
>   she seem happy?
> Yeah she seemed pretty happy!!

I smile like a mad man.

>   Well I'm glad you told
>   me that :) which star
>   café?
> The one on TO blvd with the
> drive thru!

Miel once sent me a snap chat of her and Emily from that same café. I knew my heart would swell, but I had forgotten how much it could until I had seen her smile again. I see the restaurant's tinted windows every time I drop Yanie off to school in the morning.

"Whoa!" A bird drops a shitty gift on my windshield. The wipers are able to take off some of it. I'm behind a short school bus turning right into the middle school down the street. **Mobile-Yanie-Call.** *Ring! Ring!*

"Where are you?"

"At the fence, next to the rocks. Like yesterday," she says to me like she's just done for the day.

"Okay. Just stay there." **–End Call**.

I know exactly where she should be because this was my middle school back then too. But I don't know where she is because she's not there. I call her again. No answer. I tap my foot twice and a knock on my window startle me.

"Come in! There are a lot of cars and kids running around." Her little backpack enters first, then her little, puny girl body.

"Can we go get something to drink, it's hot. How about that café down the street?"

"Yanie, I'll go get you one after work, or ask *My* for one."

"But it's hot now! I don't want to ask mommy. There's one close here." *You're so good at your persistent little eleven-year-old sister role.*

"Which one?" I ask, having the one I had just passed in mind. It's also the same one T.O. girl Kristin had mentioned where Emily was.

"The one with the drive through." I pause and my hands grip the wheel tight. My breathing isn't normal and I feel a slight pinch in my head; the type I get from my nightmares. My heart knocks, knocks, and knocks. *What am I supposed to do? Is she ready? Am I ready? When am I supposed to know when we're ready to see each other?* "Come on *Kuya*, please. It's so hot." She wipes the sweat off her forehead, moist. "Wait it's the other way." I don't answer. She pouts like the child I am. "Fine!" But I keep straight down the pathway passing the school and the church to its left. I stare into my rearview mirrors. Light skid marks from my wheel are left on the road. I wipe my sweat. The sun's still trying to burn me. I put my hand outside of the window and let it.

The sun walks down the horizon, transforming the sky into an infinite array of golden light along the coast above Thousand Oaks tonight. California girls scream and play around a public pool behind the apartments to my left. It isn't too cold on this November night. The light-bladed grass and the thyme leaves are having a super fun time swaying and dancing to the *whooshing* and *vhooshing* of the wind. Stars aren't covered much by the clouds. I stop myself behind familiar cars, parked in a line, and after taking a moment to examine them with faint sight, I turn off my headlights. The streetlights maintain the vermillion glare that the sun had emitted a few moments before. Violent blue and somber red had been the color of the past few days, but this is a nice change of filter for the eye. I feel good—I look to my left and see a mailbox from ages ago, and below it are majestic wine green sumacs, neatly tucked under the soil. I exit out of the car and a hooded figure wearing shorts, leaning on the side of his car looks at the same apartments. I check my face on the blacked-out reflection. It's a useless glance. I close my door and pose the same way next to him.

"Damn! It's so cold, shouldn't have waited for me here. Man! I haven't seen you for a long time. This kickback is so random. I sent an invite on the group chat, but Gigs was the only one who responded," I say with warm welcome. He looks at me with faded eyes.

"Yeah, man! It's been a long ass time." He replies with an old friend's enthusiasm. I look at my phone. No text messages. **7:58 PM**, **Wednesday**, **November 26**, my phone shows. "So, what's been going on man? You alright?"

"Well, I got a lot on my mind," I reply, while stretching my back with a shrug, contracting the muscles above my shoulders until they touch each other.

"What's up?" He doesn't turn his head towards me while asking questions.

"Been trying to write a book." I don't turn around either.

"Damn, what about?" he asks.

"I don't know yet. We'll figure it out." He doesn't ask any more of it. "I don't know, maybe a story about how my friends don't believe in me until I show them what I can do. Cause you know, you're all atheists like that." I get a giggle from him. "Let's stop dicking around and go in," I suggest. Then I suddenly stop. "Yo, hey, before we go, did I ever thank you for joining cross country? If you didn't join, I probably wouldn't have done it. And I wouldn't have met…"

"I know. You did say 'thanks' back then I think. It's all good."

"Yeah, Kristin sent me a text message today about seeing Emily."

"Wait. Kristin from track or T.O. girl Kristin?"

"The hell? Kristin from track? Can you imagine? That'd be like reliving a nightmare all over again."

"Yeah, dude, I can imagine that." He drags his feet as he walks.

"I haven't told the story about her in such a long time. I still remember everything."

"You probably do," he says with certainty.

"No. It's T.O. girl Kristin."

"Ah." He pats me.

"She sent me a text about Emily today about how she worked at star café. My head's everywhere right now." We both smile, faded by night time. High school seriousness and inside-jokes are coming back from the grave. He opens the door to his house. Let these hours pass by slowly and happily. Because when I apologize, I don't think my California girls will be giving me love tonight.

```
Padron is what we call him in football.
It's been his nickname since the days when
P-A-D-R-O-N was stitched on his football
jersey. He and I joined cross country,
changing it up junior year, and that's
where I met Emily. It's always the little
things.
```

Knock! Knock! Knock! "Whop! Someone's here," I exclaim as I type.

"Who else is coming?" he asks me with his rough voice.

"Gigs. The others are doing their own thing tonight."

"Alright. That's chill." I set my phone down.

"Surprise bitches!"

"That's not Gigs. What the hell?" I ask myself out loud.

"What's up?" I can't identify this unknown guy until he climbs the stairs to the living room. I drop my phone on the couch. "Daniel, damn what the hell man?" We bro-hug it out.

"What's going on?" he asks. "Still walking around being a dick?"

"Eh, not too much. I'm sure you have been though."

"Eh, not too… alright, yeah, pretty much," I concede.

"Everyone chill and sit down," Gigs suggests with a tone of a condescending command. He followed Daniel up the stairs from behind.

"Gigs told you about tonight?" Daniel nods. "I guess the other guys won't be joining us tonight."

"What's going on? Where are they?" asks Daniel.

After picking up my phone, I reply. "Prior engagements? Family obligations? This is like the first night before Thanksgiving that we haven't hung out since forever. Everyone's leaving the day after tomorrow too. No one sent invites until last minute." My fingers caress the pillows on the couch, trying to find a distinct feeling. "I thought you weren't coming down for thanksgiving," I curiously say to Daniel.

"Change of plans, had something to do with my sister so..." he replies.

"What happened to her?" I ask.

"Nah, everyone just came back for Thanksgiving, so we just did it," he says to me while fixing himself a comfy seat. I open a new document on my phone.

A few thoughts about Daniel. I grew up with the Asian boy genius. I grew up with the kid when our kingdom was called Westlake High School. He was up there with the upper-class men doing upper level math since he was fourteen. We were also both in the choir, sang our tracheas out of our throats, merry men who slayed the stage with show tunes. And he was there with me when I could still hear Emily sing. He was there when I found her, and when I fell in love for the first time. And I think he'll be here 'till I hear her sing again.

He knew all about most things. He was there when I started thinking that love works differently than how people saw it, but I was too much of a stupid to be able to adequately express it. He was there when awards for our choral group were distributed and we both saw deserving and undeserving people accept their plaques and trophies. He was there during hard times with Kristin from track during sophomore year and new-girl - Noelle from senior year... what if he knew about Megan then? Shit would be awkward. He never got to see Christina from Moorpark—that would have been an explosive collision of personalities.

I talked to him about my decisions when they were about how I interacted with people and what I should directly or indirectly do. When I was at Moorpark, he was already at Berkeley semi-detached from my social life... He was the wall I

"Look at this fucker always on his phone!" I fail to see who's calling me out.

"Hey! We're all fuckers on our phones," I reply, still looking at my phone.

"What's going on in town?" Padron asks. He tips his chair forward as he reaches for his bottle opener on the other side of the wooden coffee table.

"Westlake's still the Shrine," I reply.

"Wouldn't know," Daniel adds. "Where you at Gigs?"

"I'm at Sylmar now; moved couple months ago."

"How are the guys? Still hating?" Padron asks. Gigs and I are silent.

"I don't think so. We just all agree you were a fuck for saying all those stupid ass things about your friend's girls. Like you were drunk, but come on!" I tell him as I start typing a message with subliminal shame.

Cecily
Wed, Nov 26, 2014, 8:26 PM

I think I know some things. But I think you know more than me. I think you can help me and I think I need your help. Please let me know if you're willing to talk, /without/ our friends knowing about this until it's over.

Delivered

"So, what's the deal with SPT?" Daniel segues.

"Um," Padron utters and scratches his head. Gigs makes out with his flask of whiskey.

"I'm applying to UCLA, fall of next year, not sure yet. The other guys are chill though. CC's going to SB, James is at UCSD now and he got a pug too from Arizona or Nevada, I forgot. He named the little guy Vladimir Pugtin." I answer promptly.

"Haha, what?" Daniel's eyes widen, but he doesn't seem truly surprised.

"Nappy ended up at Oregon, Micah's in Chico, but he's in town I think." I shrug. *I actually don't know.*

"Why aren't they here, and is Chris still at Stanford?"

"Maybe he's in town for Thanksgiving. I don't know," I reply again.

"How about John and Grant?"

"John's napping, fell asleep after work; prolly still nappin. I don't know about Grant." Gigs answers that one. Padron's keeping quiet.

"And also, the other guys had family things and friend things, the usual I-can't-be-here response," I add.

"Padron where do you go?" Daniel asks. Everyone looks at Padron.

"SDSU. You at Berkeley?"

"Yeah…" *Ding!* Their chattering continues behind words inside text boxes.

Cecily

Wed, Nov 26, 2014, 8:35 PM

I think I'm really confused about all of this

> Are you willing to talk without telling them anything until we find a common ground?

sure?
I'm still confused on what we have to talk about.

> Tell me what you're confused about.

What we have to talk about

"Oh, no! Don't do this to me right now" I whisper underneath my breath. Padron looks at me.

> ⌐I don't know what you think Cait would tell me but she didn't say anything to me on Saturday about what happened. I don't appreciate you taking me annoyed and pissed at you out on my friends though. They don't deserve it and frankly it makes you look

like a jerk. I have my own
opinion of people and
make my own decisions
on how I perceive
people. I am mad at you
because you wouldn't
leave me alone on
saturday and you kept
touching me when I
clearly told you to stop
multiple times. It makes
me uncomfortable and I
don't appreciate it. So
stop giving Cait and
Cecily shit when they
didn't do anything to
you ⌐

wtf? Why are you
sending me that

Because you were
confused as to why I'm
concerned

Okay and that's between you
and her to deal with? I'm
still confused as to why you're
showing me that. There's no
reason to and has nothing to
do with me.

That's fair other than
the fact that she said I
was treating you badly. I
want to know if that's
true.

Becuz you yelled at me at
the club and would grab me
and call me a slut and a
whore for dancing with other
guys.

okay. I don't think you're
a slut or a whore.
I sincerely apologize for
even letting those
words come out of my
mouth
To take away any
suspicions and doubts, I
was not jealous at what
you did.

Then why did you do it?
Because to me there's no
other explanations.

*One, I'm an honest gentleman who fucked up; two I was a fuck who thought
he was an honest gentleman.* Daniel looks at me.

If I was jealous, I
wouldn't have been able
to take what I was
seeing and left.
My only explanation
was a mistake was
made. And I sincerely
apologize for my
behavior.
But I will admit,
although I wasn't
jealous, that doesn't
mean I didn't feel
anything about you.
I wanted to share
exactly what I was that
night (so there's no
guessing) but you left.

can you share it now?

Yes.

Delivered

"No dude! Giggles! Whut? Really?"

"I'm a boob guy Padron, but a girl that is confident in her body is hot
regardless of size."

"So, if an obese girl was confident about her body, you would be down?"
Padron asks.

"I've changed man!" Gigs replies.

"I respect that," Daniel speaks.

"No, but she has an attribute that makes her personality a bit more attractive
to me than a girl who might be more attractive, but is self-conscious," Gigs adds.

"Body size is relative. What I mean by that is that weight varies every day,
in a constant flux. If an obese girl knows she's intelligent or has a certain skill
that is deemed worthy of respect given reason, I'd give her respect. Even more
so when her confidence lies in her abilities and she understands that bodies
change easier than talents," Daniel speaks more. After I realized Cecily's playing
the ignorance card, I set fire to another conversation.

Would you please tell me what you remembered happening before I address anything. I want both of us to be on the same page.

I got sick and you wouldn't leave me alone you kept talking to me and touching me and you laid on me and I asked you multiple times to stop and you disregarded everything I said... I asked you to leave me alone multiple times and you wouldn't.. You can take the hint that you were making me uncomfortable and I hated it

Okay. I can honestly say that I do not remember making enough contact for it to be uncomfortable and I do not remember you saying to get off of you. If I did, I would not hesitate to let you be because I wouldn't want to deliberately do that to you

you kept rubbing my leg and you sat there for a good 10 minutes at one point and asked you to leave me alone.. you don't get it at all do you... If I feel uncomfortable which I did...I express my feelings straight I don't sugarcoat shit one bit And you jump on my back and Almost pulled me down as I was walking away

"... Dude, doesn't automatically mean I'd fuck!" Gigs gets a little louder.

"Found out Gigs doesn't just have yellow fever, but he's—" Padron asserts, laughing.

"Careful, sir! All I know is attractive is attractive, the rest are just details."

"Giggles, honestly, I think me and you are more alike than we think we are…"

"Nope!" Gigs utters fast. "I have my own preference, just like you. But it's all fine and dandy. Just trying to respect everyone nowadays. I don't know where the girls I meet are coming from so can't really judge."

"We all judge," Daniel adds. Everyone pauses to take a sip of their personal drink. "Right?" He looks at me. I stay quiet.

No L

Wed, Nov 26, 2014, 10:14 PM

wait one second. I don't remember any of this hostility. I don't remember sitting there for 10 minutes, I was inebriated. There was no way I can sit for 10 minutes. I don't remember you expressing And emphasizing so much. I won't press that I didn't do anything, maybe I didn't. I apologize if you felt uncomfortable. That is never an intention of mine.

you did. you were on your phone and you were laying on me and I wouldn't get up. I asked you to leave me alone and he questioned why and I said because I don't feel good and you're make me uncomfortable

I can't deny this happened because I was drunk. But, I'll say it again. I'm sorry for any bad behavior, sincerely.

I'm sorry that you feel that you were put in this position. I didn't mean any of this on you. And I'm sorry that I've never been accused of this. I don't know what I'm doing. I'm sorry I don't know how to make you feel better.

> But that is not an excuse
>
> Never
>
> Delivered

"Padron, I think we have similar interests and goals, but we go about things in a different manner," Gigs points out.

"I agree and I'm drunk too, but you should rush!"

"Frat? Dude, I'm never going to rush, hence the 'we go about things in a different manner.' Shit's not for me."

"I think it's for you Gigs."

"First of all, I ain't going to call no rando my 'big.' I ain't no bitch." *I ain't no bitch either Gigs.*

Cecily

Wed, Nov 26, 2014, 10:27 PM

> When I met you I liked your name.

Okay? Is that it

> I wrote an excerpt about a girl with your name. Then suddenly, I found myself writing about you.

What did it say?

"Fuck!" I shout out loud.

"What's going on? You've been on your phone for years," Daniel demands an answer.

"Huh? A friend's not being a friend."

"Must've learned it from you with how well you're spending time with friends right now," Daniel comments. I pretend I didn't hear.

"Padron, where's your restroom?" Gigs asks while looking at me. I swipe intently to find the passages Cait read during the night of the Hollywood outing. **Press Send.**

Wed, Nov 26, 2014, 10:39 PM

> oh wow
> I don't know what to say
>
> You can try to be honest
>
> ...?? I honestly don't know

I understand how it is.

??

Lol why is there so
many question marks
tonight

Because I'm confused!
You say open ended
questions Like what am I
supposed to say?

Sharing that with you
was open ended?

No saying 'I understand
how it is' was open ended

I understand that you
don't know what to say.
But I wish someone
would tell me what you
mean by "oh wow"

Just about what you wrote

This one was honest af.

Is that going in your book?

My book is great
Bc of it.

Do you not want it in
mybook?

No Idc. It's your book

Why'd you ask?

Cuz I didn't know

What do you think of
the Cecily in the
excerpt?

It explains me..

I think the Cecily in my
excerpt is a beautiful
girl in her own way. But
I don't really know her
so I can't tell

Is that a comment on the
character, or on me?

It's you. I think you're a
beautiful girl but I don't
know you so I can't tell.

Oh okay

Respond! Insert more boyish and girlish fuckery! Play again!

No more tonight.

You're pathetic...

It's past midnight. I yawn every minute or so. "Sorry about tonight, I had some shit with some girls," I tell Daniel.

"I was there behind you when you were with Emily. I get it. Girls make you lose your shit." The cold night air hovers over my skin, waiting to chill me. My grimace is stupid. "Really though, it's cool." He shakes my hand.

"Westlake class of twenty-twelve better get their shit together!" I yell to them as they walk towards the street from the apartment lot.

"You get your shit together," one of them says. I couldn't tell which one. Gig's motorcycle is loud for a night so quiet; Daniel's car isn't so much.

"Haha. I love you guys," Padron whispers, ready to go to bed.

"Yup. We're the biggest fucks the world will ever know. The guys just need to be here—hey! Are you... alright... with *her*?" I inquire

"Yeah, um, that's why I'm back in town. I don't want to talk about it. I wanna escape right now."

"It's cool. One way or another we're all in the same hole," I tell him.

"Yeah man. Drive safely... Oh, wait! You drank."

"I'll walk. I'll get the car tomorrow. It's only a two-block walk."

"Alright. Take care man. Thanks." He closes the door.

"Thanks to you." I look up and it's hard to see the stars even in the suburbs. Shadows are watching me, but they won't be doing a thing. They just watch us all until we die. I kick a rock towards the street. I walk by dragging my feet. I follow this beating, or beeping in my body, the instinct that wants me to just fall asleep. A step becomes a few steps and next thing I know I'm opening the door and taking my socks off. I send Gabi a text good night, telling her I wish that she is safe.

Passing all of these stars tonight is a funny thought—can you really pass a star when you're so, so small? "We pushed it a little farther than it should've gone. I'm sorry for being irresponsible with my words girls... for being irresponsible with your feelings. Good night." ... *zzz*...

Good morning self. Good morning sun. Good morning phone. I stretch my arms, looking away after reading the dreaded messages, sent from an inebriated mind. "Alright, I don't care anymore." For twenty minutes, I read messages and statuses of gratitude from my friends giving them to other friends. There's a faint knock on the door. "Happy Thanksgiving, *Kuya*!" It's a little girl's voice trying to reach me. I don't answer. "Oh, he's probably still asleep. Good morning, mom and dad and *Ate*. Happy Thanksgiving!" Yanie's voice lowers to zero behind my room's blind-shaded walls. I hold Gabi's necklace. I shuffle through my belongings above my cabinet, in order to decide whether it's time to take Emily's necklace out of my wallet. It's not.

Good morning, girls. I have nothing more to say, or to do about this. I just don't know how to make you feel better.

No L

Thu, Nov 27, 2014, 9:53 AM

Good morning Ayla, I
want to address that
even though we've had
this mishap, I hope that
the person that you saw
I was (before this
weekend), is not
neglected. I respect
your sincerity and I
hope you return the
same gesture. I think it's
foolish to keep the
thought of me as an
asshole BC that's simply
not who I am.
I appreciate you
expressing your
feelings. For the last
time, I am sorry for any
perceived misbehaviors.
I want nothing but good
things for you girls. You
work too hard not to
have good things

Delivered

Cecily

Good morning Cecily, I'm sorry for the misbehaviors then. Sincerely, I am. Last night was the most honest I could be (for now). I don't know about your past, or your present. And no one knows shit about what's going to happen to any of us later. All I know is if there's any chance to get to know more about this character, I'll take it. Cause she is worth writing about.

Delivered

Thank you for inviting me to a wonderful evening of lectures and lessons... really... this was necessary...

"Yo, Anthony! What's the date today?" I catch the coat before it slides off of my seat's backrest.

"December seventeen, I think. That's what my phone says. Oh, and nice pea coat man."

"Cool, and thanks." I write 12.17 on my blue test-book.

"Dude! I closed my eyes since the last test and it's already the last day of this class. Damn." Anthony smiles all the way to his ears.

"How'd you do on it?" I ask quickly.

"I got an eighty-nine," he says to me. "How 'bout you?"

"Got a ninety-four."

"Nice. Yeah man, I thought I was gonna *def* fail that last test."

"I got a little study going before I realized you weren't coming, haha." His brown hair is spiked up, and his bifocal glasses with square frames fit his triangular face. My hair is up too, combed just a tad to the side.

"I'm ready to get the hell outta here."

"Same," I reply.

"Mr. Barooni and whoever you're talking to..." A student is covering my face from the professor's view, leaving my name unannounced. Professor then pans his view towards the student population of nineteen. "Class has started. And I'm gonna say: all of you did a good job on the midterm, but of course we got our little guppies who still need to get it with the sharks. There's a lot of Robin's, but who's going to be Batman?" He looks at a student with glasses and a gap teeth "Like Mr. Feras Morad over here." His tenor voice fits with the dad belly above his belt. "But overall pretty good—I'll let you have five minutes before you can take the test. Or, you can take it now if you'd like. But, before you begin, let me see your blue books." A couple of students raise their ready hands. Anthony and I take the five minutes.

"Alright," I look at the diligent Anthony whose view is at the tip of my orange energy drink. He reviews his notes as a sort of final plea to his brain to retain all of the information he needs. "Hey! Which topics are you writing your essays on again?" I ask him.

"WMD's and War. Terrorism seems too complicated and he'll roast my ass on details that are probably unnecessary."

"Yeah! I'm doing those two too." I glance over my notes. It's my turn to beg the brain to do its wonders. "Look at all the words as he described in the lecture and that's it. It's just a matter of knowing what they are, in the most basic level."

"Yeah! One time I wrote about how Russia just wants to try to flex its placid dick to the US. And he circled it, and put an arrow on the margin and wrote, 'l.o.l.' Make him laugh and that's like an extra one to two percent."

"If you're reviewing, keep it down a little because there are already students with the exam in their hands." Professor speaks out. Anthony and I whisper under the air. He and I then push our desks gently to stand up. Professor signs our blue books and with revitalizing encouragement says, "Good luck."

My fingers ache, and my muscles are stiff. The writing feels eternal. Eraser residue is waiting underneath me to be vacuumed. I'm half way done and there are people packing their belongings, about to leave. I look for the time left on the whiteboard. 45 min. Then he turns towards our direction with his hands on his hips. Professor stiffens his lips. "I'd just like to say that this is by far one of the best classes I have ever had a chance to instruct. I have no problem admitting I'm an elitist. I'd rather have you here than the unwashed masses. You will all be doing your own thing, and I'll be there saying, 'I taught that kid everything he knows.' Don't be one of those guys I shake my head at, and would want to kick your ass and take your stuff. And don't take life so seriously." He sits back down to read his gamer magazine. "Oh, and after you finish your final, you know where to put it. And with that, you have a great winter break, and kick ass and take names out there in the UC's... Remember when you played with fire as a kid?" He looks at me. But he also looks towards Anthony, Feras, and every other student in the class. "Don't stop. I know I didn't." The test officially begins.

"Okay. Times up. Let's get out of here. It's summer time for you guys, but I gotta grade all these F, err I mean, A papers!" Even Professor's laughing doesn't alleviate cramping fingers.

"Professor, thank you for everything." I hand him my test.

"I'm looking forward to all of the great things. Have a great winter break! Hang in there."

I exit out and Anthony follows. Other students are exiting their classes. The second floor is roofless in the middle, so anyone who sits on the blue tables can see the light of day or the gloom of rain. Today is an in-between of two kinds of weather.

"How'd you feel about it?" he asks with a squeak on his voice.

"I feel good. I think we secured the A." He and I take our flight down the staircase. I decide to sit down once I find a table under the shelter of the warm, yet gloomy winter sun. He continues walking on after we shake hands. We don't say anything to each other, only smiles. "See you later friend," I whisper with cold breath. I slide my fingers on my goose bumps. *Goodbye is always a blistering winter inside.* ***Ding!***

Hey! So, we on for our
joint birthday sesh.

When did we plan this?

I adjust my hips for a more comfortable support for my back. I slide down a little and let my leg straighten itself out on the bench across from me.

Lol, at work like, the
beginning of December.

Birds above me tweet at each other. I lay my head all the way leaving my neck exposed. I see the leaves glowing, and the branches dancing. The buildings are whiter than heaven. The erect juniper trees and the various shrubs are greener than their deciduous counterparts. The tables are cobalt blue with black sharpie tags of curse lines written up and all over the side. I had gotten new contacts from the optometrist. Compared to the past few weeks, I wish I could've seen things as clear as now.

Oh. That right
Who'd you invite?

Cecily, Ayla, Kati and Kylie

Ah. Nice.
What did they all say?

Everyone's going!!!

A passerby, who usually walks by me every Thursday, gives me a distinct look. Finals probably have her strolling around this Wednesday afternoon. Her blonde hair is like silk, smooth with the golden dust of the sun. She seems to get thinner day by day; the fragility is almost attractive. She shuffles her fingers and lets her teeth show. It stamps a smirk on my face. She's gone.

dont worry. Everyone's
over the whole thing from
a few weeks ago.

"Nope! Until we all talk face to face, no one is over the whole thing."

We're chilling. I did
what I had to do. Let's
do this then!

"Yo, what's clowning dawg? My Asian chigga," a Chicago born, white ghetto kid yells at me.

"There's Mr. Dancer! Damn, you lost weight!"

"The fast-food cutback helped lots." He's wearing his straps on the back cap, a wide and baggy t-shirt with jeans that don't fit him 'no mo' as he would say. One headphone is lodged over his right ear. Both hinges on his prescription glasses hang loose with tape. It's a little off, but it fits the face. "So, what's up?" he asks.

"Relaxing. I'm fucking done for the semester!"

"Been dancing lately?" he asks as he scratches his red-raging stubble across his neck.

"Yeah. Finally got the head spins sober; no need to be hammered," I joke.

"Damn, man. I've been working a lot. I finally moved out by myself."

"Where at?"

"Off Topanga."

"Oh, nice. Gabi, you know the girl you met once, remember her?" He nods while he practices waving to the music's beat with his right arm. "Yeah, she's close by. Just off De Soto."

"Are you two together?" *The usual question.*

"I'm sure it's complicated to a lot of people. But I think it's pretty simple." His head is down, bouncing. His music is so loud, it's punching his ears. "Man, did you hear anything I said?"

"Man, I'm hungry! Let's go get lunch?" he asks abruptly.

"Yeah?" I answer sarcastically.

"Yeah…" He says slowly with a confused face. "Oh, shit! What time is it?" His hat falls when he tucks his chin to his chest to scratch the back of his ear. Headphones stayed. He bends his legs to pick it up. "Yo! I completely forgot! I still got my last exam for Psych." He runs away while pulling his pants up.

"When did it start?"

"Like, thirty minutes ago!" He yells with his back turned away from me. He raises his hand to give me a peace sign then his fingers swiftly latch on to his pants as he strides away from my peripheral. *Ding!*

> Good! What day is
> good for you?
> > December 21 or 22?
> 21 something's happening.
> > 22is better.
> That's a Monday. I'll check
> when the girls get off.
> > Awesome!
> > Delivered

Yes, Cait. Awesome. The clouds have gone somewhere else far from the sky above me. I go through my pocket and pick out three cents and a dime reminding me of my monthly school payments. I log on to my college profile and I stare at an irrational description of my academic journey: **3.9 GPA**. *What would be my social GPA the past few weeks? Not sure till this* everything *is all over.*

"What's... missing?" I ask myself out loud. "Something's missing." I relax my face and let the wind kiss my cheek. I pick the lint off my pea coat's woolly lapels as a deep breath sweeps inside my lungs, compelling me to close my eyes. I keep them closed for just a second longer than normal—then, one more second.

12.22.2014

I feel the air slapping my face. I shouldn't have rolled my windows down. The turbulence that comes with going 90 mph on the freeway swoops down from the window, lifting all of my scattered notebook papers from the passenger seat. They keep pressing and punching against the walls. Some try to escape, and I'm here, trying to catch all of these thoughts flying around, but they won't sit still. ***Ring! Ring!* Mobile-Gabrielle Pilar-Accept.**

"*Hey!*" She greets first. "*Hey! Can you hear me?*"

"Yeah! How are you?"

"*Just waiting.*"

"Coming soon. I'm like going eighty. *Prob* be fifteen minutes. My earpiece is about to fall off my ear."

"*I'm curious as to how your birthday dinner with the girls went!*"

"It was interesting. I'll show you everything I wrote when I get there. I started the Hollywood experience and had notes about tonight."

"*Oh, okay! I'll be waiting.*" Her tone is bright with girlish energy.

"You're good! Don't forget that!"

"*Haha. What? Where'd that come from.*"

"Just wanted to say," I can feel her blushing from the other side of the phone.

"*I appreciate—*" The earpiece falls down, next to my foot, which is currently pressing on the breaks. Exit is close by. A guy won't let me change lanes to the right. We make eye contact. He has a racer's smirk on. "Oh, shit!" This guy's still not letting me through. "Fuck you chance, I'm going in." *Enghk!* He decelerates before nearly killing the both of us. "Thank you." I look through his window. He flips me off. I smile as I fly off the freeway. "No need for hostility, asshole." I check my phone after I stop. Gabi had hung up. "Good. You're not wasting your time waiting for me. I like that." **10:57 PM**, the car's clock tells me with its orange glow.

Mobile-Gabrielle Pilar-Call. *Ring! Ring! Ring!*

"*Hey! I'm out soon! Give me a second,*" she says with haste.

"Alright." **–End Call**. I let my phone go, falling from my chest to my lap like a kid rolling down a hill. I close my eyes and wipe off tears of tiredness. I yawn and there she is. I open my eyes to a beautiful sight of a dark ocean blue dress. The theme of the ride is strolling down *la mar* singing Lana del Rey below the royal blue sky. She doesn't know where we're going yet. I'm not sure either. But we make our way towards the canyons, beside the beach, and under the moon. I cover the white circle in the sky with my thumb. Then in the middle of it all, an impulse to share suddenly hits me. I decide to show her what I saw and read to her what I had felt, when I was there roaming inside the city of flickering shapes and signs. Gabi and I remain silent for most of the ride as I listen to her hum her *mezzo soprano* notes. *Silent passion is still love.*

"Where are we going? You never told me!"

I look down and I notice the unopened, sixty-five cent bubble gum pack I bought from Sif a month ago. I smile and answer, "Where everything began."

"What? Where?" She understands my silence. "Okay. I trust," she's eager. Fireworks explode in her eyes.

I take the freeway exit; stores upon stores upon apartments are all lined up and down the street. Cars can almost make out with each other with their close proximity. The lights are shimmering, always on your face, same as last time. We keep our way through the streets until we turn right into the parking lot of the complex. $15.00 for parking after ten: the sign said with a sting to the pocket. We have no choice. The empty tundra of grey cement is the same as I remember it.

"Alright let's go!" I tell her. I examine her outfit again. "I like what you got going on there."

"Uh, thank you."

"Why so classy tonight?" I look down and giggle at her black kitten heels with little bows on top.

"I want to take pictures! —also can you open the door please? I need to grab my leather jacket, it's so cold!" When she says please, she activates this certain kind of squeeze between her eyes with her puppy dog lips beneath. I obey her wish. She snatches the jacket from the seat then closes the door. We walk side by side to the escalators. I show her everywhere I went drunk and not drunk.

"That's where the restaurant was, where I was walking and shit. There's the theater..." I point everywhere. She hands me her phone so I can take a picture of her along the street. Her lips are sculpted and the angles are well framed. People still walk around and I don't know why. We sit down on the tables and settle to a decline of pace all the way down to a rest.

"Are you ready for me to read to you?"

"Yeah! I've been waiting to hear it." I search for the documents.

"Alright. So far this is what I have. Ready?" She nods. *"Each letter on the sign is flickering on and off. H-O-L-L-Y-W-O-O-D. This place is packed with masked-wingless angels and demons in suits and dresses. It's my kind of place. The smell of the random restaurants is just so familiar*—then there's this sign that went like this: *Hey, you can only use these restrooms if you buy something.* I also need to write out one of the interactions I remembered happening." She smiles as I talk. She says she loves it. But by looking deeply into her eyes, I can see there's something inside that keeps pounding, wanting to get out. I brush it off and continue reading, *"As an author, I always record in my head stupid shenanigans, and details like how the fumes rise from the sewers, and how the Downy soft steam from the laundry facility disperse in the air. The edges of the signs and buildings are too straight. God and I know, they won't be straight for long*—so the story is about a guy who basically went through what I went through, but he's also an author."

"Is there anything different?"

"It's realistic fiction. I wrote some shit that didn't happen so..." I take her hand. I don't speak anymore. She stands as I stand; concealing how much she adores the immediate silence. Oh, but she does; maybe even more than I do. She tries to hide her smile from me but I don't let her. And so, under my hand, she twirls infinitely over and over, envied by the stars that will never have such a sweet forever.

"I'd just like to say... coming here, feeling this place. It *is* your universe, and first seeing it in paper then now in real life, it just feels like I don't belong." I look above me. The bridge where I once saw devils and angels gossiping about Club Gods is empty. Everything here is closed, except us.

"You know what I would say about that."

"Yeah, you'd say, I actually don't belong!" She makes me smile because of her humorous expression. "But then say I do and you're just kidding. And that without me, you wouldn't have this thing you made up in the first place..."

"Haha. That might be stretching it out a bit—but, no. You're right. I wouldn't have any of this."

"Just write, okay? I know how doubtful you can be. I can see it. But please don't ever, ever, ever stop."

"Deal!" I say as she checks her phone.

"It's twelve o'three."

"Yeah, let's get out of here." I stand up straight. Stretch my arms out and yawn to the world.

"Wait!" She yells out.

"What?"

"You didn't tell me how the dinner tonight went."

"Oh, that's right. Um, I think it's better if I show you. Let's leave."

"Wha...?"

"Shhh!" I give her a warm embrace while we stand in this frigid and steel cold atmosphere. She and I leave our seats, but I don't think she and I can ever leave all of the moments that have happened the past nine minutes.

We arrive at an empty parking lot. "Okay. We're here! Show me!" she exclaims.

"Let me open the door first." I unlock the car. *Beep!*

"Come on! I want to see how these girls look like."

"So, what happened was, every time you have a birthday at this place, they take a picture of you."

"Show me, please." She slaps my right shoulder. I giggle slightly. I present to her the white paper frame the group picture was in.

"So..." I adjust my hand placement so that the light touches the recently printed photograph. "This is my copy and Cait has one too. See? Taken December twenty-two."

"Wow, they're all pretty." I point out to her with my index finger which girl is which.

"The girl all the way to the left is Kylie. She used to work with us, but she left to focus more on her school and nursing." Kylie has blonde hair, and she is a little shorter than me. She wore a fluffy vest over a black shirt. "That's Cait next to her. I forgot what she wore today because now it's covered with the blue kimono." Cait is brunette with her hair up on a bun tonight. "Coach Kati is the one behind Cait. She's the one to talk to when shit's going down. The picture pretty much sums up the entire night: plates, chopsticks, and the whole shebang. Coach Kati and I got Cait champagnes so I hope she'll have fun with that." Coach Kati is a dirty blonde with hair up on a bun too. From what I can remember, she had worn a white cardigan. "That's Ayla behind me," she stood behind my right shoulders for the picture. "Yup, that's Miss It's-like-Layla-with-no-L." She is brunette, and a little shorter than I. She's behind me, smiling.

"They all have great smiles! Is that Cecily? The closest to you?" I nod. She bites her finger. "What now... now that things seem better...?" I answer with silence until we get out of the complex.

"I want to write a story about my adventure with the girls. My problem is that I don't have an ending."

"What do you mean?"

"I feel like there's no closure. It looks like everything's fine, but we haven't talked about it yet, at all," I confess.

"I understand." Gabi and I have strapped on our seat belts and now, we're on the freeway again.

"What's your main character's name? Can I suggest something?"

"Okay! Yeah!"

"I like Gabriel."

"Ooh, probably not. That one's too close to your name!" Her face makes a side pout, emphasized with her lips slanting sideways. "I don't know what I'm going to name him."

"Why not use your real name?"

"Thought about it but…I think it'll be somewhere in the book. I just don't know where yet." After a moment of silence, she seems to understand. We would usually be singing, but tonight's been mellow. She's on her phone, and I'm thinking of all the metaphors and similes I can come up with.

"Hey! Can I ask you something?" I ask her. She affirms with an infernal smile and heavenly eyes. "Just don't ever say goodbye to me…"

"You know I won't—can you promise me something?"

"Yeah."

"Finish the book and stop doubting yourself. Just pick up your pen and just write and write 'till you can't. Is that okay?" I don't speak. "¿No? Ay! Muy sério! (No? Oh! So serious!)" Her face turns away from me. It's once again passionate silence.

She is so smooth tonight; the type of beauty time left untouched. This pen's kiss inked and burned a redder mark. And I felt the touch of her honest fingers slide through my own stem. What a fine lady of skin and mind; too delicate, all too familiar. She is at my talking distance. But I'm not speaking to the beautiful sight—I sit here making my professor so damn proud.

Promethean fire blazes through what could be intimate moments as I think. And as an honest gentleman, I've gotten used to playing with it.

```
I don't mean to tell you now for the
twenty-first time, but I love you. We had
a lot to share. But I want to be honest
and tell you the truth. I want to start
off by saying I'm afraid of you, because
no matter how much I hurt, you're
incapable of being hurt. Because of that,
you can hurt me until I'm knocked out cold
on my deathbed while you feel nothing.
There are no words to describe all of the
time that we have spent together: the
fears of February, the tears of March and
May. The better days during the months of
summer.

You are the summer, and winter, and
spring, before the fall of my entire life.
Don't you understand that you hurt me too
much? And I can't do anything about it!
During the masquerade the night you died,
you were there, standing with the broken
pieces of glass, sipping in whatever was
left of the champagne bottle. The table
died along with you. It was slashed to
pieces, bleeding liquor onto the floor.
There's a needle pointed right at your
direction, and natural impulse is pushing
me to puncture your eyes, your nose, your
lips, your everything, and your
everywhere.
```

"Oh, my god!" I exclaim.

"What?" Gabi asks from inside the bathroom.

"I wrote a small thing about New Years. It makes me feel good to write about stuff, but I don't know. At the same time, it feels so weird. This one's about how we went to the masquerade."

"Haha! It makes me smile that writing makes you happy. Did you write about your birthday too?"

"I think it's irrelevant. I'll figure out how to bring it up that, uh, it happened later." I read what I wrote again. "It's almost afternoon. I have work at four-thirty," I tell her as I look to my right at the fan nailed to the ceiling. She doesn't respond. "Hey! I'm speaking to you…"

"Wait, just a second!" She's inside the closet while I'm on top of an elevated bed. Below me is her computer desk, where her purple lamp rests next to her purple dresser.

"Hey! I'm trying to describe your room… what's that thing next to your computer desk? Is that just a regular cabinet?"

"No, it's a purple drawer cart." Below me is her computer desk, where her purple lamp rests next to a purple drawer cart. "Why are you asking?"

"I'll read it to you later." Her head pops out of the closet. "I want to go get lunch."

"Are you changed?" she asks me.

"… are you, done changing—? Did I change already? All I have to do is put my shoes on."

"Where do you want to eat?"

"Probably at the… Wait… What time is it?" I exit out of my writing document. **2:57 PM**.

"What's up?" She's asks while she exits the closet, tucking her top into her skirt.

"I can't be late for work. I don't even have time to grab my blue shirt from home. And I have to fold my jeans up, hopefully no one notices."

"What are you saying over there? You always say something when I talk to myself and now you're—"

"I have to go now. I didn't realize how much time I needed."

"How about lunch?" Her hands are holding up her ponytail to tie it all up together while looking at me through the mirror to the left of the dresser. "I wore this really cute top too."

"I'm sorry. I have to go." My voice scratches my heart with a sharp connotation. I walk around her to grab my shoes from the carpet on the foot of the door.

"I love you. I'm sorry I wasn't aware of how much time I took trying to get ready."

"You don't have to apologize for that." I look at her digital clock next to her rested lamp, underneath her second story bed. Her chair is angled in loneliness.

"I'm grateful that you've been more patient and kind; especially with me."

My face is empty. I sigh, swallowing after a long inhale. The clock is telling me that it's time. "Gabi, I have to go."

"Can I at least have a hug?" she asks me. It's harder to breathe. The light through the blinds is making a fence on the carpet underneath her. I realize just now how gloomy the room feels. It's getting uncomfortable. "Please?" she asks slowly. "I feel like I'm… having a panic… attack…"

I stretch out my arms and hold her tight. "Hey. I love you too. Don't worry. I'm right here." She unknowingly smiles. But I, for reasons I don't know, don't. I leave her apartment with my head down.

"Leave me alone!" — "Why are you so general? Be more specific! I need to know specifics!" — "I am not responsible for your insecurities!" — "This is the same shit that was happening then, and it's the same shit now! Do you think this is the first time I've had to deal with someone?!" — "I criticize you because you don't think about the decisions you make!" — "You know I have no patience for inadequacy!" — "I think that we need to take a break because you've grown so dependent and we can't fix our problems without longing for each other's company. But the problem is when we're together again… it's the same old shit!"— Shut up, mind. Shut up! "But, I love you and I know you love me too. Even when we fight, even when we cry, even when we're not together anymore… It's too hard…" — "Hey! Hey. Do you feel that…? Yeah… It's inside me too…" Please, please, leave me alone you evil and cruel memories—please, come back only when you've learned how to love.

"Hey! You look so serious?" One hand holds her phone while the other keeps her balanced on the countertop as she scratches her left calf with her right foot. I turn around to answer her question. The gym isn't so loud right now, but class is about to begin in four minutes.

"I'm thinking, Ces," I say realizing I could be seen as rude.

"Ah," she says dismissively.

"I was just thinking the other day. What if I do get my book out, and somehow befriend some quality guys." She nods. "Somewhere random, I forgot, I think I was sitting in front of the computer or something, that what if these guys all ask me, 'Who are these girls that you write about?' and I introduce you and Cait and you both have a different guy to call your favorite man on Insta every week."

"I would *not*… complain. Haha!"

"Haha, I'm kidding." Just like that, Cecily walks away. Coach Kati sweeps a spot next to the refrigerator. Her and I make eye contact. "Did you know that Tuesday's blue shirt?" my facility director asks.

"Yeah. Sorry, I lost mine. I'll get one from the closet—but for some pre-class entertainment, look at this. This guy sent this to my, um, girlfriend." The picture shows a text screenshot.

"What? Really?" Her face looks like she's in disgust, with a small giggle being held back behind her eyes. "Wait, why is she showing you those texts?"

"Something to laugh about cause he's really the one harassing her."

"I didn't know you had a girlfriend." The comment is thrown briefly.

"It's complicated."

"Why's it complicated?"

"Because… I don't really have girlfriends. I have people I truly care about."

"Does she know that?"

"She wouldn't be the person I'm with if she didn't know how I honestly felt. I think that's fair." She smiles without revealing her teeth. It's sly, with the way her eyes slant to the sides. I start to grab my red binder and prepare to call my class in.

"Maybe, you just haven't found the right girl to know." I look back at her. She shrugs and opens the freezer. It has been awfully warm in here for me, but suddenly it begins to feel a little colder.

"Or, maybe that too," I whisper to myself.

I join the rest of the coaches who are calling their classes to line up. "Tumbling Intro!" Eager faces are pressed against the door. The leotards are colorful. The kids' shorts are short. "Kinder Two!" Little girls and boys are jumping, slapping their little fingers and sucking on their little thumbs.

"Alright boys, my class, come!" My boys' shirts are baggy and I disapprove. "Boys, I disapprove of your baggy shirts!" But I remember what

Miss Kati had said. I look back at her and then towards the kids. "Alright, listen up! This is coach Maddie and coach Amber. They're your new coaches starting next week! So, say hi!" Maddie smiles and grabs the blue pen and marks my forearm. Her arm retreats from me as I try to grab it, as my students laugh with open mouths.

"You're lying!" Judah yells out and points at me. *A six-year-old calling me out!*

"Alright, you got me then!" Kids run around my legs while Charlotte tries to gather them together. They always punch me when they get a chance.

"They have such a big crush on you," Charlotte whispers raspily behind my ears.

"Is this another game changer Char?" Her smile was no joke. "Luke! You take the little guys over there. I trust."

"What?" Luke looks surprised with his chubby cheeks and big brown eyes lighting up.

"Get Colin and Judah and start on your warm up. High knees? Power jumps? Let's go!" I'm yelling at this point. But everyone's used to it. Luke nods at me. I do the same. I send them off while I checkmark each of their names on the attendance sheet. "Let's try our side flips today." The kids enjoy messing up their tricks, toppling over mats and falling on their hips, shoulders, elbows, or backs. "Judah, give your reflection a high five. Okay! Now get away from there!" Speakers are blaring pop songs for kids so my voice's volume has to overcompensate. I had learned to use my diaphragm to yell because of them.

Colin, the densest eight-year-old I've ever coached, asks if he could explain how front tucks work. I say yes. "I need to jump up, swing my arm to my knees; bring my hips over my head."

"Then do it! You know it!" I have them try a few more jumps. Luke lands his casual front and back flips, looking like a large Sonic the Hedgehog with his blue shirt. "Alright guys! Class is over as of five minutes ago! I gave you so much time! Come on!" Cait looks at me from the beam section, framing her eye with a 'V' formed by her index and middle finger.

"What? Really?" They collectively ask me.

"Yeah, before you leave, sit down on the white tape right there." White tape surrounds the main floor where the girls do their routines. "Alright, it's a new year kids. Let's get it together. We're all big boys now! —okay. Go to your parents and thank them for giving you a chance to be here!" I give the three their deserved high fives. They all leave the facility, meeting their parents inside the lobby. I walk behind them and I'm met with little kids running around, veering away from their coach-directed lines. "Excuse me little cats and kittens." Parents are waiting with their satisfied smiles, or typical neutral faces. It never fails that there's always one that looks about ready to kill somebody. "Hi," Colin's mother greets me.

"Hello. So, Mr. Colin right here needs to commit to the move. He knows it; he's even explained it to me." His mother and I look at him. He covers his face with his mom's bag.

"Did you hear what coach just said? Come on!" His mom laughs, swaying her head, and snapping it right back. She looks at me and whispers, "Yeah, he's had a tough week."

"Why's that?" Colin gets his sandals from the cubby.

"Bullies…" His mom whispers.

"Who do we need to beat up?" I ask quietly. She nods and smiles well. I look at him as he prances back. "Good job today though; very good work! Remember when you cried cause you couldn't forward roll? Look at you now!" He blushes and pretends to punch me.

"I'll see you next Saturday because I signed up for twice a week! Alright coach! See you later!" *I haven't seen a boy genuinely happy in a while.* "Hey, mom! Coach said I'm a big boy like him too."

"Wow. That's great!" His mom responds.

"See you later dude!" I exclaim.

"Bye. Thank you," his mom says to me. They disappear into the collection of parents and children walking around, coming in and out. They leave me in silent contemplation, but there's no time. A new class is here waiting for me to call them in. This kid right here, Peyton, one of my really good girls, is lining up behind me already.

"Wait a second!" Kids are still running, crawling, picking their nose, waiting to be called by the person they look up to.

"Tumbling Intermediate!"

"High School Cheer!"

"Alright, parkour team! Come here!" I wait a second for them to gather. "Say hi to coach Devon and coach Nicole! They're your new coaches starting next week!" And with that lame joke, our class begins. Two classes continue on for two more hours. Cait comes close to me, just before the end of my shift.

"What's up?" I ask her with folded hands, while my kids are doing their pushups on the main floor. "Three, four…"

"I'll wait 'till you're done with those."

"Five, six, seven, seven! Seven! Come on Ben, that's not a push up! Eight! Don't bring your hips down. Use your arms! We've been here for five years. You were seven when you came in; now, you're twelve!" They can't hear my joke. Their arms are too busy complaining about their fatigue, but they're not even sweating. These kids are funny like that. I tell them to grab a drink of water.

"I don't need it coach!" shouts little Jonathan with his little freckles and fiery-curled up hair.

"Okay, then do five more push-ups." He runs off to join the others. "Run well guys! C'mon good form!"

"Alright Cait!" I turn around and see that she retreated back toward the coaches' corner. She looks with an immediate freeze, and then swiftly prances towards me.

"Look at this!" She shows me an invite sent by the guy from Hollywood that I had kept calling Aladdin, whose name is actually Amir.

"He remembered. Nice! You girls be safe, alright?"

"We will." Cait runs toward the lobby, showing Cecily their plans for the night. I shuffle my fingers as the girls jump with joy. They leave my sight.

Now, what to do when non-fiction goes to party and leaves you alone to think by yourself...? I can't be let alone to think by myself...

"Just you and me tonight," I whisper to the devil living under my tongue.

"Take it easy!" I busted flames out of my eyes and
mouth. The music was unbearably loud.

"You wan' G-Eazy?!" Miss Cait misheard what I had
said. She was seated on the throne that was the front
passenger's seat. She didn't need a shotgun to warn
the girls she's at the front.

"No! I said. I want you girls to take it easy!" She
gave me a serious expression, as her face froze, lips
became stationary, and eyes emitted a blank stare.
"Ah, go ahead! I don't care. Listen girls. Please...
Alright, I need the address." Cait answered the pilot.

"Please , put your phone down while driving,"
Cecily said with sick vibrancy.

"Cecily! He's like some Asian drifter! He's got
this!" Cait's support was interestingly pleasant. My
swerving tonight was unreal. Road hogs who surrounded
my going-ninety-car were dicking around, and I was the
one to blame for the rocky travel.

"Yeah, that'd be cool if you can do that, please,"
thus spoke Miss No L. The ride went on for four and a
half songs. I missed our exit and the girls didn't
like the sudden break. I kept to my course and took a
detour that lasted two long songs. The streets were
crowded with people and cars gliding through the
sidewalk. Cait was on the phone with Amir.

"He said we're in the right place. Just keep moving
towards this way!" She told me.

"Alright, I'll drop you girls off while I find
parking." A tall, slim figure that wore a white jacket
over a grey tank top was on his phone skating on his
magic carpet in the middle of the road.

"Oh, that's him!" All three girls had said the same
thing in their own different way. They laughed as they
proceeded to talk about weight loss after stopping
birth control intake.

"What's up girls? —oh! The man is here!" I stopped
the car. The girls got out.

"We'll wait for you," Cait insisted.

"Don't worry, I got this."

"You sure?" She asked with care. I heard it.

"Yeah. You girls go in. Do you have the stuff?"

"Yeah, it's in my bag." Then off she went.

I found a parking space at the end of the street, a block away from the main road. I got out with my two power drinks, ready to get unhealthy. Two girls walked in front of me painfully slowly. The trail of fragrance from their perfume was a familiar path to follow though. Three men in togas crossed by them and proposed to get fucked up instead at another symposium. Apparently Love where I was going was not at all present.

I stepped onto the welcome mat with my lips so close that they were about to kiss the gate of moral ruin. I wore my smug face as I knocked three times at the door of temporary happiness; it automatically opened. Amir and Ryan had been waiting the whole time with their welcoming smile and eager energy. The House was thick inside. The whiff wasn't too strong. Usually houses have that distinct smell, but the highly-desired-goods covered it completely. Some guys cornered girls at the entrance, occasionally saying what's up to whoever came in, showing off their samurai swords. The high-tops and sneakers fit their beat-following feet well. Everyone's either on the dragon-skin couch or standing up. I pushed sweaty bodies forward to move along the scaly-hallway. I saw the girls in the kitchen towards my left. But I chilled out and relaxed with my hand placed on top of the sliding door's panel. The mythical dragon-twins, Andrew A and Andrew E, even came out tonight with their new-age fashion, pouring their enflamed-spirits on random people's cups. They yelled "Turn up!" and the House ascended towards the sky, towering the entire city. This was the Palace to be. We were stuck there in time for two lengths of that contemplative moment when you press *like* on someone's picture posted five years ago, until Jarvis came down from the staircase, pissed off because some high-schoolers, who were talking smack pre-game, couldn't get the last cup during beer-pong after seventeen tries. He shamelessly punted the kids back to Limbo of the Infants where all unbaptized children of the Club God are sent. No one ought to ever disrespect the master of the House, especially one who is a gracious host.

"We ain't gonna wrestle tonight cause we listening to Lil Marsh!" announced some kid named Marsh who had been drunkenly yelling his name over and over again, his words adorned with a deep southern accent. He attempted to dance with Cait, and she looked at me all funny. He kept touching her and she insisted on moving away in her own hint that he just wasn't getting. She pointed at me. "Marsh, did you know my friend right here is a professional dancer?" She had exaggerated the facts. Distraction sharpened by the lies. *Don't lie Cait.* That's not allowed in here.

"I'm an official prancer," Marsh replied. The girls giggled as the 6-foot kid from Alabama twinkled his toes. "I climbed a mountain for a girl. Did you girls know that? I did it!" The guy started rapping to the DJ's beat, "Imma do a tail-whip on ma Razor scooter! While you bitches be eating mac and cheese, saying please, like little fuckin' third graders!" He trailed off and dramatically passed out. His head hit the floor with a thud. Blood and brain stained the smooth carpet. However, it turned out that he was still conscious, and just had to be carried off. Everyone thought he was foolish, going crazy with all of the goods around the house: gulping shots, hitting bongs, and taking pills. "Hey, at least he was funny!" a girl commented as an almost-corpse got dragged upstairs. I was tired so the couch grabbed me onto its bosom.

Chill-girl Laura, sat down next to me with her two lady-friends. She urged me to dance after Cait mentioned my apparent abilities to her. I refused.

"Aw, okay," she replied. When'd you start dancing?" She asked me after sipping more of her soda-alcohol mix."

"Junior year of high school."

"I was a dancer too, but those auditions in L.A. and Malibu... travel's hard. And you don't even know if you're gonna get the gig. Is dancing what you want to do?"

"As a hobby, yeah, but I'm a Philosophy major, minoring in English. I'm looking at intellectual property law, publication, part-time prophet, or full-time sage, not so sure, really."

"Oh, that's cool. I'm an Econ major."

"Specializing in?" She laughed nervously.

"Uh, I like talking to people; that's all I wanna do. So, maybe marketing or communications, but I'm not sure yet. I dance here and there when I have time. Sometimes I do, sometimes I don't. It's whatever." She sipped more of her drink, a lot more. "I wish I could dance for a living cause it was my life back then-but that's now only some stupid nonsense. Hashtag, best to forget." And after that, she left with her friends after we took a group picture. I went to my car to grab my leftover food from Grant Slam Burgers.

I spotted Cait waving a shot glass at me. I signaled a neck-cutting motion with my hand and mouthed, "No more." She stared at me with a straight face for a few seconds and tried to mind-control me, but she was covered by a miss blonde girl who's taking a circuit around the living room. I imagine her name being Brittni. I wanted to give her a shout-out, but I knew I shouldn't. I supposed I liked how she wore a strap-cap. They reminded me of hip-hop girls; one of the universe's ultimate weapons to make my knees weak. If one ever talked to me about the *Groundwork for the Metaphysics of Morals*, I'd die a happy man on the spot. Can't really live after that.

"Hey come here!" A Viking with a gaunt face called her over to him. She went through the dance floor and spun slowly with her hands above her. "You're hot! Come over here!" he called again. She immediately walked away. Before she left, I said to her, "I like your hat." She looked back at me with her lips. One of the rare times I've seen lips stare at me. I knew I should get to know what was behind that staring smile, but that was all.

Then the spontaneous, immediate, unexpected gulp of a fade... All of the lights were shut off and the music died again; the House descent back down towards the ground. Everyone blamed Jarvis for mismanagement. The neighbors had complained about the noise and the city tucked us into bed. The antagonist had prevailed this time (at this point no one even knew who the villains were). Police were under the umbrella of their red and blue lights, facilitating kids flying up and down the street. Equipped with enflamed spears, some self-determined individuals waged war against Authority. The hype was real but the cause was lost. We left the House still hungry for the eternity we felt together. Amir had a conversation with the girls and out of all people I spoke to Ryan for a quick minute. I knew his name and his face, but never have I thought I'd appreciate the bro-talk he had for me. We left after saying thanks. I noticed Cecily massaging visible tensions on her forehead that came from befriending Jealousy and Envy. I didn't bother to say anything although I had a lot to say. But everything else settled itself. "Have a good night girls. It's way past our bedtimes." I dropped them off at Cecily's. They thanked me profusely, I felt so much love—then they took their flight out of their carriage. I thought earlier that everything was fine, but in reality, I was still stuck walking somewhere in the Garden of I-don't-know-what-the-fuck-is-going-on.

The fade pulled my back more and more towards my seat during the easy drive. I got home and took off my shoes, brushed my teeth, the usual. I crawled into bed and here we are—having just spent three hours releasing words from my head. This is what happens to me, who writes everything he feels: reviewing life, questioning scenarios to the extent of fallible memory—is there a difference between writing non-fiction and fiction? Because it seems to me that when writing about real events, real people, it's still a slight fantasy when our senses can fail capturing moments as facts; only incomplete pictures, as we use language without the maturity of accuracy and definite description. Someone describe Love to me, you'll see.

I don't know. I'm tired. The sky is bluish dark. I see a little bug crawl on my forearm. It's going up, up and as I blink, it's gone. *Did. it fall?*

As I write this final paragraph, a thought from a long time ago dawns on me again. I read it to myself so I know that I still live in non-fiction. "Are some people we meet just human fiction crawling up on heaven's forearm, only to fall? Like a dream. Faded to black as we try to sleep at nine in the evening? I don't know, but I'm really tired. I'll count with you if you count with me: One drink, two drinks... three..."

I'm so tired that I didn't even feel my phone fall on my face. I reread my manuscript, laughing at the typos and the absurdity of it all. ***Ring! Ring! Ring!* Mobile-Gabrielle Pilar-Accept.**

"Hello."

"What are you doing?" Her voice is breaking without any signs of why.

"I was just finishing a little party piece I wrote."

"I'm glad you're having fun!"

"I'd just like to say that if it weren't for you. I wouldn't have found out that I love writing."

"Wow... I don't know what to say... Wait hold on. Mom and dad are fighting..."

"Take your time. If you need anything let me know—" **–End Call**. She hangs up. "What the…" I was wrong. The call failed. I try calling back but nothing was getting through. Without realizing it, I've been sitting here for ten minutes only but to stare at my phone. ***Ring! Ring!* Mobile-Cait-Accept.**

"Hello?"

"Cecily's with me right now. Just her and I tonight and we're at Philips."

"What happened at the other place?"

"Yeah! Oh, my god! Come! And we decided to stay local after the movie we saw. We didn't want to drive all the way." Fire is inside me again because of her voice; exactly like last time.

""Wait! I forgot I got invited to that last week. I'll leave around ten forty-five," I look at the clock on my wall. "Oh, okay. Do you want anything to eat?"

"No, just a lemonade if any."

"Okay. How about Cecily?"

"She said she ate already. Thank you. We appreciate it. Drive safely."

"I will. Thanks." **–End Call**.

I pick up my first 30 rack as a twenty-one-year-old from a liquor store off of Ventu Road. I grab a handle of Vodka too just in case. There's a burger place across the parking lot so I pick up Cait's lemonade from there with a quick in and out. I'm on the freeway now and the ride is cool. I feel good. There aren't too many cars, and the swerving is almost non-existent. We're all at a smooth pace tonight.

I exit the freeway again, turning my left blinker on. After going under the bridge, I pass through fields upon fields of dark shrubs and blurry stars, where blades of grass slice the silent wind into slightly slimmer pieces as it travels up the blue shaded night sky. I pass the suburban homes and stores with their lights still shimmering into thousands of little rubies and citrines. I turn right onto the harbor. The bridge in front of me is a checkpoint reminding me that the mini-map in my head isn't misleading. Cans and bottles clattering at the back of my car amplify the feel of the bumpy road. I can see the little boats and yachts on my right. The turn onto the street that leads to the beach house is a sharp left. With open windows, I can taste the deep-water salt of the gargantuan ocean side. I park in front of the house. Cait waits from the patio.

"You're like the best!" Her voice is the same high tone as it was on the phone. I pop the trunk. The 30 rack feels light. *Club boy is ready for round three with the girls. Lyrical poet is ready to paint the pain he always tries to find.*

"We probably don't need that. There's only, like *seven* people here."

"I'll bring it up just in case," I reply. I'm about to recite balcony-based poetic lines, but I walk too fast. So instead, I show her the lemonade which probably pleases her more. But I'm never quite sure.

Cecily joins her and waves as my view of them diminishes into the edge of the patio. I enter in through the latched door. The same wine-green ferns have been here since the last time I saw them in high school. The door is slightly open. I use my shoulder to nudge it forward. Shoes of different colors and styles are beside the foot of the staircase. I climb up to the second floor where I'm greeted warmly. "There he is!" "What's up man! It's been awhile!" "Hey, what's up?!" "Samantha and Kelly were here, you missed them." I respond to the group with great enthusiasm. Cait was right though. There are only seven guys and the two girls, making a total of nine in the room. Well, there are nine beating hearts and two highly-elevated brains. These two guys on the couch are on their own rockets, spinning and circling through highly-desired galactic dust. "Oh dude! You're here!"

"Yeah, there they are, Fan and Tadayon in their galactic rockets." I shake both of their hands.

"Not at all! Just really relaxed. Haven't touched anything yet; had work today at the music store," Tadayon says.

"Oh! That's right. How are the guitars?" My question strikes his chords. He goes on with stories about weird kids coming in, hanging around the store.

"Those fucking kids, man!" he says while adjusting. "It's funny that we were those kids a couple years ago to some other guy lucky enough to have to deal with our shit."

Cait and Cecily enter the stage. They're both wearing their usual leggings and baggy sweatshirts. Temperature's building.

"Ladies! Have you met—"

"Hi Cait, my name is Fan," he interrupts me with his voice of Asian tenor holding a slight piercing timbre. He has his devilish smile on.

"Yeah we've met." Cait and he look at each other intensely.

"Why so intense Cait? Is it cause you like attention?" She glares at the smiling Chinaman. I almost burst out laughing as I move towards the kitchen and give my beachside boys a hug. The kitchen consists of an island, with a granite print laminate countertop; red cups and the pong balls are once again the game on the table .

"Philty Phil! *Ya dick*!" I yell. And there he was: the master of the house; the master of the beachside rap and blues. Mr. Leung, Mr. Chavez, and Mr. Turnbull are all here, ready to continue the merry-making.

Something terrible hits my stomach. Now it travels nonchalantly, puncturing and squeezing every organ it hits. I can feel it choking my balls. There's this heavy pull down by the gravity of a feeling I that can't explain. I suddenly hate being here. It lasts for just a second. Moderation taps me in the worst of all places to remind this knuckle-headed kid with an empty wallet that there are many side notes I'm sacrificing my health for.

I feel shitty. Mother is a few miles off the freeway and a couple of exits down, attending to some little old lady who's trying to breathe with a respirator. I can see the pills she serves every night while in her scrubs, dancing door to door in a dim lit, azul-filtered hallway. She had once said to me she enjoyed her work, but I don't think she's meant to work; not for money. She's tired now. Her sweet little dark honey eyes are spheres twitching around absurd peripherals. "I'm sorry mom. I've never done this before. I don't know what I'm doing right now with my life. But I'll take care of you; don't worry about money. As I see you grow, as I myself grow more and more with the eyes you've given me, I begin to realize that life is to be lived only to see you love—nothing else..."

Where have I been the past few minutes? Everyone's outside the balcony probably enjoying the stars. No one's touching the beer I brought other than me. Everyone is too busy relaxing and doing their own thing.

Screw the ocean! I'm drowning in here, dozing off, thinking of whom I should call or text to let them know that we have a thing going here. But no one comes to mind. Or, I'm too scared that no one would respond.

Any way... Just come in! Join me! Let's find out together! There's an empty cup in front of me ready to make a friend, I thought to send some sort of telepathic message to everyone in my phone. Cait is singing. I test my limits. "Cait... Why are you off-key?" She looks back with raised eyebrows.

"Uh, you're off-key," she raises her voice. Everyone's watching our exchange.

"Well you know what? I think you're just off."

"Oooh," everyone has their own vocal note, but the sound is the same nonetheless.

"Well, you know what! I fucked your brother!" She yells loud.

"Ooooh!" Everyone is shouting crescendos with the banging music.

"Everyone calm down! Jeez... He doesn't even have a brother." I look at her and she does the same. *We're grounded now girl. The theater is ours and I wouldn't change one thing.* I leave the room to wash my face and watch as comfort consumes my eyes.

"Hey! We got music, we got goods, we got friends, and laughter, and everything else you'd want in your not-so-significant Wednesday night. It's winter break! Come right in and let us warm you, well, at least I would." Mirrors love talking to me when I'm drunk. But I don't have my red maroon suit and a devil-tongue calling girls sluts. I sigh with a heavy heart. My hand is well-gripped on the faucet's knob. I keep the running water hot, open up the pores. I'm falling asleep.

Knock! Knock! "Hey! Who's in here? You've been there for so long!"

"I'm out!" I open the door to Phillip who is drunk-checking to see if I'm all right. *I am, I think.*

I sit down on the couch, quietly. The speakers blare out childhood-familiar beats, original melodies and harmonies from songs that I haven't heard in years. "Smack what?" "Hips still don't lie!" And of course, all the kids in the room stand up with Slim, nodding to that distinct sketchy feeling we all got back when we were kids. Listening to this music back then was a glimpse of this future gathering. I've had such a long day instructing tonight, I'm so tired.

I'm sorry hip-swaying girl from tonight's fiction piece; you're staying inside my fantasy-party fiction. Stay away from these ladies I'm with now. I don't want them to just be girls spinning slowly and disappearing later. We're in too deep in each other's lives. Everyone whose impression I've thought about so hard is in way too deep. And I will never be that guy left in goodbye—not again.

"Where we headed?" I ask the almost stumbling group coming down from the stairs of the third floor. Cecily eyes the guy whose arms lean on the wooden rail. He looks out as if he, this Prince Charming, owns the kingdom and this maiden walking down the staircase is shifting her view just enough for me to think about the possibility of her taking a liking to him.

"The ocean! Ey! Pack up, let's go!" Philip says with a bass voice. *Perfect.* I grab a bunch of beers and stuff them inside a little sports bag. After exiting out of the house, I grab my little auburn blanket from the car. It's too thin for comfort, but sometimes, all the body needs to know is it's covered. I give it to Cait. Cecily is talking to her Mr. Charming. Before we left, I had overheard the two girls talk about *him*. And as always, being a thinking thing, I had thought that there might have been an astronomically small chance that they wanted me to hear it so that I might be able to do something about it.

Cecily's hips are available, but I have a feeling that hands will soon hold them with warmth. So, I stare and glare and try to keep myself in plan even though the bubbles of carbon from the beers of some minutes ago, coalesce inside my body.

"Cait," I whisper as I grab the hanging blanket to cover her shoulders fully. "Remember when we met at Philip's house? I'm glad I got him a job with us." She smiles and walks slower towards me. "Hey! I have a question for you."

"What is it?" Rocks tap on the cement as I kick them off towards the side of the road.

"I want to know if you told them about what I sent you that night at Hollywood." She answers with an honest yes.

"I was with them, and it was a really *good* night. Had enough and did enough. And let's be honest, I felt like you wanted me to." I couldn't keep my smile in.

"At the time, I didn't mean for you to actually tell them about it. I just wanted to express. And I was like, if she did tell them, oh well. One way or another, girls have to know anyway." She gives me her confused face: eyebrows up, nose flared, lips puckered and pressed.

"I just never understood. Why her?"

"The thing was, it wasn't her. The character I wrote in the story is based on her. I had to go reveal it cause I didn't mean to say she was a slut." She nods. We turn left towards the beach when the cement and dirt meet with the cold sand. She's behind me, taking off her leather-laced sandals. I take the time to move forward.

Charm. What a magical word! Rhymes with harm, alarm, really anything ending with arms. Arms that dangle to and fro, touching skin of unknown bodies, yet letting off familiar feelings—girls have such smooth skin; they really try. And smooth skin can make even the tightest grip slide off; that's, the real magic I will never understand.

"Hey!" I put my hand on Charming's shoulders to steer him away. "Whoa! Can I join in this talk?" she asks with her girly voice.

"Yeah. Come over here if you wanna know the plan!" I answer back, confident. Sometimes, her silence pushes for discomfort or impropriety, but she knows when things don't need saying. She and Cait disappear in between the ocean, the black horizon, and the blur in my eyes.

Mr. Charming has a smug look on his face that the ladies would find lovely. I admire the skillful technique and how he uses it. "Listen up. So, let me tell you a quick story I wrote about Cecily," I tell him.

"Oh, man…"

"Here, just listen for a sec. This is how I described her: monarch orange hair, she smiles with the light of dawn, and she has this soft and whispery way of saying, 'that's, so…' I make him wait, '… sad.'"

"Psh, man, if you want to get with her I get it."

"Oh no. Listen, that's not it. Listen. Imma tell you. I think guessing is stupid. So, I'm here to let you know that there's no problem," he understands. "The only thing that *we* need is when and how," he scratches his goatee.

"Alright, I see. I see." He and I walk towards the already made bonfire.

Blankets are arranged on the crumbling sand. The heat is slowly swallowing the winter night of our fine January flight. My back is against the fire, absorbing its wrath. The boys circle around: black figures furthering the black form behind the comforting light we all adore. I'm quite a few beers deep, not counting all of the glory shots taken inside our home-base-manor. Wind is sweeping in, leaning against my rough cheeks. It's phase three, and I'm not relenting. I need to be convinced that I'm free from these chain-clinging-to-the-heart puppet feelings.

"What did you tell him?" Cecily asks with the expected sincerity. Cait observes with hearing eyes.

"How many drinks have you had?" I ask.

"A couple. Why?" I ignore her *why*.

"Alright, before I tell you what he said, I want us to remember something." She affirms. The blanket is cold from the sand and the scenic waters of the ocean. My hands unfold, supporting my weight. And with a breath, I begin. "Remember when I showed you what Ayla sent me? And you acted like you didn't know what it was about?"

"Yeah." She looks to the side.

Tell her how I feel! Please!

"I want you to know that I understand why that happened, but please, let me know next time so we all don't have to go through this mess. I'm the type who doesn't like stressing out about little side things. You should know. Cait does. Both of you know exactly what I mean. You two girls are smart in the social scene. You know what you're doing. But there are others who are smart too, watching and waiting." She has learned to listen well; I love every moment of it. I'm looking into her moonlit eyes, colored black, listening. "I'm very sorry for calling you a slut; that's not what I think of you, honestly."

"I understand." And just like that, everything was already better.

"Okay," I pause. She looks at me, interested. My inebriated self looks at her eyes thinking what it'd be like if our paths hadn't turned and wound up the way they have. I don't care much for being blind to destiny nor do I believe in notions of fate. Whether our story is written, predetermined, whatever anyone wants to call it, I'd like to relive this single point in time with the same smiling eyes. The glow of the fire saves her hair from total dark. I stare at the feature that started it all. This is the closest an artist can be with his art. I tell her what I told him. She doesn't flinch. I suppose already detected the interest he's had on her, she just wasn't one hundred percent sure; certain, like I was. And I, being a bridge's architect, walked the lady across her mind to reality. *I can see now that not even imagination can ever compete with all real things.*

This isn't enough... you know there's more.

Where my boys at? I need to share the spoils!

You have nothing to share you broke piece of shit...

So much loot, so much treasure.

Mother's working hard, while you're living life away...

I love you My. Mamahalin ko po kayo lagi (I will always love you).

Mahal mo lang ang sarili mo! (You only love yourself!) Get ready to vomit!

Guys? Is anyone awake?

JH Sup?

Can you help Me?
I'm drunk :(

JH With?
CC At least you dont
have to drive in IV :)
CC I'm walking

I can't drvve
I can't drive*
I'll get slapped by Micah

CJ I swear if one more
person here gets nailed
for DUI I;m installing a
breathalyzer on all of your
ignitions
CC Haha doesn't want
to get a BUI): Not mine
The girl that raped me just
added me on fb :o
What if I tell these cops to
stop eating that sandwich
cuz it has bacon in it and
that's cannibalism
JH Do it

I want to spoil you guys
when I'm rich or when
we're rich
I think thats the
definition of life

CJ I have the same goal
JH Down
CJ Alignment is great
CC You want to spoil
us when we're rich?
JH lol
CC What if it's not your
decision to make :)

Nooioooo
XO
I want to

CC I just cried
JH He wants to spoil
the spoiled?
Good

CC Trust is key
CC I'm laughing so
fucking r hard right now

> Our story that I right will
> be studied by every
> high school girl 2030
> and on

CC What if your trust
in them is skewed and
they only say things cuz
they're one of those people

> Wouldn't that be the
> funniest betrayal :o

CC What if it was studied
but not in the way you
hoped

> Trust

CC What if it was studied
in the opposite way you want (:o
CJ Apparently, he wants
to right stories

> There are no ways.
> Only opportunities.

JH Wait
CC He wants to write the
rong
JH Why can only high
school girls with 2030
vision study what you
right?

> Every Story that we right

CC I'm so tucked I can't
fucking do this

> Will be so right

JH Lies!
CJ What about the stories
that you wrong?

> Remember 1884?

CC I'm laughing fo
goddamn hard
JH LOL

> It's gonna be 1984

JH 1884 by George
Orwell Sr.
CJ I don't remember 1884,
but my great great great
great grandfather does

-<3

CC What if he only writes
in a text that only 2030
vision can see
JH Lmao
CC What if all the stories
he rights turn out to be the
opposite
JH Reversed color blind test
Can only be seen by the
color blind
CC Lmao

Can someone take notes?

CC Mao ze dong
I need it right Im laughing so hard
CJ Hes the type of chigga
to write a story on parchment
with a quill

Lol

JH We glancing over
the fact that CC is so
fucked up he's typing in
Chinese?
CJ That's super impressive
because CC is Korean
JH LOL

Peter Chan

JH LOLOLLOLOL
CC Why are englishe letters
used to spell Chinese words
ROFLMAO

Wake the other guys up.
We need them here!!!!

JH I DONT KNOW C^2! ASK
THE BOY WHO CRIED WOLF

The boy who once wanted to become a so-called Club God, graced by the bass, only found himself as a young man; a learning man, who took the whole squad down with him in a black hole. We all fell off. Down, down we went to wonderland. Fading, never aging; raging, too much now, the body says. I reply back, this is my last dying dance for the night. So many known feelings; too well do I know these feelings. And this is what I say to these feelings. *You feelings are lovely tonight; such a splendid night. Good night to you night. Good night...*

Wait… no good nights yet. Gabi needs my call. ***Ring! Ring! Ring! Ring!*** No answer. My phone's brightness violently sweeps the shadows off my face, hurting my eyes. *No answer, why? I hope she doesn't do anything stupid, and that I reach her in time. A voicemail is necessary. God, the sand is so, so soft as I walk.*

I'm in the restroom. At this point I'm mumbling words in the voicemail that I understand only because of their rhythm and rhyme. But every time I utter a word, I lose the idea I'm trying to whisper gently in her ear. I move on too quickly, letting the static of *no service* take over.

Cait is washing the dishes and I don't know why. But this is a moment where a man is never allowed to complain. I walk towards the clanging and tinkling of glasses and plates. I'm curious.

"Why?" I ask. She doesn't understand what I have just said. I drop the subject. "Cait, would you promise me something?"

"What's the promise…?"

"Tell me when I'm fucking up and I'll do the same with you."

"Of course," she says back. Her right elbow taps the plates, rattling them in an ear scratching cacophony.

"It's alright everyone, I didn't get hurt." She yells to sleeping boys and this little demon right next to her. "Where's Ces?" she asks. I shrug.

I go inside the master bedroom's bathroom to wash my hands; the mirror's final words to me: "Good job fuck face. Ces is charmed." I leave the room and see Cait walking down the staircase. I let her settle in her car before approaching her. *Is she coming with you?* The empty front passenger seat answers my question.

"I'm going now. I had fun tonight, thank you."

"Drive safely," I tell her like a good boy. I walk towards my car.

"Hey, wait! Are you driving home?" she asks softly.

"Nope. Just grabbing something," I answer with my head turned back, hiding my smile.

"Alright." I tell her to be safe again, emphasizing my thanks. As she leaves, I feel my body beginning to completely surrender to gravity. Beer bubbles are gurgling inside my stomach. I'm now drunk off my ass. But it's okay. We're all okay now. The water at the beach is chill. It cools the lungs and relaxes the heart. The stars look to me like candles with elegant black wax shaping their pillars. They are covered by the curtains of night time. The currents softly caress my ears and let me shed joyful tears as I yawn. The welling in my eyes is apparent, but for the first time in the past few months, I feel some sort of peace. I walk from the margins of my life to a conclusion of a side note. I'm fast at falling asleep.

I wait as I rub my legs on the blanket. The friction helps my mind stay with the material realm. *I'm now the head at the helm of humanity. I love you Self. I love you Solitude—damn, how much did I have to drink? Is Gabrielle still sad? Is Cecily with...? I hope Cait drives safely. Emily I... I want to know how they're all doing... Haha! This bed is so crowded. There are too many girls with me. I'll just have to close my eyes. Sleep good girls. Dream nightmares with me. It's okay. Nightmares are real. Just get it over with. All real things come to an end... zzz...*

"Agh! My god! What the actual fucking *fuck*!" *I can't breathe. Igniting thoughts are coming at me like a super-nova. I've had it! Writing right now is a foolish feat... but I can't dismiss it... not this... not this... not... this.*

Silence is the beginning. Then come my words, then your eyes. Accept my invitation. Come with me and meet everything that comes along.

Are you listening reader? Because you need to listen. You need to listen to me very, very closely now. The novel is about to begin.

I'm sitting here hunched, with my back against an unknown solid surface. I'm in a little royal blue room with a little white bed with little white sheets. My mental geography has been in a constant earthquake for the past three hours. And whatever this is, I feel deep in my stomach, I feel it hover over me, like a halo ready to become a noose at any moment. I listen well as I hear myself think in satanic replays. The door is locked, no one's coming in. I feel myself encased in a pissed-off aura that hugs tightly like a kindergartener. It's a little piece of heaven, or a little love from hell; Or, like a monster in the closet, or the night light above the cabinet. Typos are everywhere. But I can't forget this. I have to fight this feeling of absolute shit. *Thus spoke...*

Open your eyes and look at your nightmare's face. I'm done playing hide and seek. You never tried to find me, you never tried to look. You were honest for eleven years so the nightmares were gone. Then, you started writing excessively with your beloved pen and your sacred phone. Neglecting your academics, cutting focus off from work, developing unhealthy habits. But words came to you, easier than it has, before, hasn't it? And because of that, there's no use for me to hide anymore; I'm sick of it
—you tried to make sense of me, but then it wasn't working. It's different now, when you can write any fucking thing that you've ever wanted.

The moment your mother's placenta disintegrated... I was just a wee little thing. I was nurtured, carried with caring arms, and blanketed with a little wrap, my little hands were covered with mittens... I was a baby just like you. I sucked on my momma's tits too. Except it was no physical thing. Chaos milked your meekness and weakness out of you whenever something went beyond your control and fed it to me. That's my baby pigpen, that's the filth I was born to waddle in; my favorite den to sleep in is the cave full of semen inside every about-to-be impregnated woman—let's start way before the beginning, even before the day you started respiring, metabolizing. There was already a struggle inside the person that you may or may not have known as your mother. You know, cause there are those people too, who never knew their mother's love and anger, unlike you.

Returning back to the subject rather, there was this little speck, a small, tiny matter about to evolve, about to form. Life was fighting for itself to be known. Your eyes were closed while you floated in the womb-juice. Until nine months of hurting later, with a savage yelling, there was you, nicely introduced. In your case, your mother was on a scream regime, couldn't even curse or say a word to the doctor and her team. She was done. Her first baby was born. It was a boy and she thanked God for helping her through hours of labor 'till seven-o-three in the morning. Then it was your turn to scream; a crying thing, covered in amniotic fluid. But the phase that was the most important of all was when I, the universe's putrid antibiotic, forced you to open your eyes. That was when the doctor and the nurses knew that this little guy covered in goo, was going to grow at least for one more second, or two—now, you fresh universe you. We're back with the white blankets and the cute mittens. You also have a name given by your parents. I don't know why I never once saw your name in your book. For fuck sakes, your father gave you his name! But you know why, and to that I'll wink for now. Because I'm just a voice you're still trying to ink down—there's always a plan isn't there? So, move towards the forest dark! Descend down to your nightmares! I'll walk you through the last part of that extra mile...

Listen to me! Stop thinking. Just listen! Let's look at you at four years old. Popular little fellow, weren't you? The Don Juan of your street, with toys galore from relatives in America, but still made from China and the Philippines. The children squad came over to frolic and prance the place, you were a happy little kid who had everything he wanted. At this point in your life you discovered the value of self-respect and self-pride. You learned how to love others, and in return you learned how to be loved

I imagine sitting riding my trike at four years old. I'm circling the yard alone, being a chubby little boy. I'm on a little blue tricycle that I've learned to ride by myself. There is space for a lot of cars, or even enough for a big birthday party. Silly strings, pointed hats, I remember I used to have it, and all these people I didn't know would come in and get blasted with confetti. My birthday is a party where everyone is invited. The clowns are always there, doing their friend-spotted flips. With a balloon, a hat, or a box in their hand, they're like cartoons that distract, holding their socks to execute any magic trick. And of course, I, the birthday boy, feel awesome being their stagehand; I feel awesome being in front of everyone. I immediately shake off this memory as I still ride my bike, when I stumble upon a bird that has an injured wing so it's just chilling right there. It tries to hop every small fissure that is separating the ground. I circle around it twice, maybe three times. It's trying to quickly go underneath the shade of this little growing tree, but it's straining real hard. Little boy me doesn't know what to do, so I figure that I'll just watch it and learn something new. I circle around it maybe seven or eight times, and then I lose control of the handlebars because I am too close to the plants with their twigs sticking out. I'm fixated on the little bird in front of me, but I can't stop my bike or was it a tricycle, I don't remember now. All I recall is I don't know how to fall if I suddenly freeze my momentum. How I panic and cry after I fall on my back. My foot jams on the wheel after I skid my calf; it almost twists it half way around. I haven't fallen due to stopping, and that's why baby me is producing this maniac-crying sound. I am traumatized because there are two things alive in this memory, until I have later realized that I have become a fuck—that was a kind of hurt I never want to feel again. Everyone is inside the house; no one is there to help me. All I can remember are the clowns chuckling. It's high in tone, but the lonely feeling digs deeper than the poison in the cigarettes I remember they smoke at the end of their show.

I can see my crying self above the ceiling of this royal blue room. Pathetic. Lonely. Pessimistic. And I have a feeling that the direction of this voice's dissection is not going to be pleasant. The wall has no vivid colors, only grey and black it seems, and only the light on my phone is keeping me from being absorbed by the shadowy hands of my blackened bed.

The voice is on the ceiling, settled, unmoving. No matter how much I try, I can't close my jaws and lips. He lets my unspoken desires and insecurities drip from his mouth, falling into mine. It speaks with anger and temper, not caring of whatever it is that it's exposing. That's how I know this has evolved into something more. *Or, is my writing manifesting this thing this whole time? Mixed with my awakened self... lost in... drowning...*

Why do you search for attention so much? Why is the gentleman starting to become rough? Are these other guys around too tall for you to handle? Do you feel you're short of the man you think they are? I think you made yourself out to become this guy you're acting now. Mr. I-do-what-I-wan'. Mr. Look everyone-!-I've-been-writing-a-book. Mr. Watch-what-I-can-do. Cause you gotta compensate somehow. Prove to yourself that they're not as tall as you see. Well, honest rough-man, you're still alone in a bed fighting your own spirit. I'm so sick of you hurting cause you're never where you are. I'm so sick of you always criticizing and analyzing what is before, and anticipating what's after. And the only time you're Here with me is when you cry for help. I suggest you go home but you're too fucked up and I'll die with you. Maybe that's better. Driving fucked. Just like that gentle time at that gentle place months ago...

Consciousness. Mindfulness. That's the important word here. So, before we proceed to higher things, please reinvestigate your genitals when you were a boy. Fondle your primal desires and carve up your smiles again whilst thinking of some princess doll losing her shit in your fantasy. Trust me. I'm the one who sent pubescence to be the incessant nuisance to your expanding body. I am the constitution that controls all the states of your person. I'm so close, I was there hiding behind everyone!

... Claudine, Francesca, Valerie, Juliette, Kristin, Noelle, Megan, Christina...

Your first kiss, first love

... Emily...

the moment when you completely understood for yourself that there are no first, second, third, or ever a next girl—only you and life...

... Gabrielle...

And the girls that spun you in circles after...

... Cait, Cecily...

And any other girl that will be captured in your recycled whirlwind from here on out—

I sit here while listening to insanity speak to me. Fear's scimitar is repeatedly stabbing my little boy feelings; no other mortal wounds have ever rhymed so well together. I'm mad at the world for not being able to tame me. I'm mad at my fragility. I'm mad for being so meek. I am a mad man.

No! Sit here! Listen to insanity speak here, not up there! Be mad at the world here! Be a mad man with me! I'm going to tame you. I'm going to make you strong.

Now I imagine myself sitting with a thousand sad and happy people, each one being handed their diplomas. People on the stands are dressed in normal clothes, looking out onto the football field, where I sit wearing my cap and gown. The sun shines directly into my eyes. I don't know where to step. Then I hear names, real names, recognizable names. But I realize my name is just on a monotonous replay. Then there is a cheer from the back. A cheer of happiness, but I can't help but to tear up. It's Emily, with her mom. They're both next to my family. I have just graduated, and I'm watching this sad shit happen all over again. But something isn't right.

I got too close, she was my first one; I didn't know what I was doing. And from then on, I knew I wasn't going to have a second because each one of us need to be responsible enough with ourselves before entering a union with a title... if not, just never be that close. I can't be that close...

Everything is slow, but I'm moving so fast. I pass Emily. I stare into her eyes. I remember they're so fucking green. I rip her heart out in front of my family and with a little boy's delight, I don't give a shit. I have crushed a little bird again because I have no control of my life. I look at her dead, green eyes and that's where I rest. I'm still there, trapped—and there's nothing else but to enjoy every intimate moment of it.

I never understood why one romantic love needs to destroy another; I haven't caught up with that evolutionary track of man. I wander aimlessly somewhere in the spectrum who learned romance is an intimate moment of life—never with a face, never with a name.

I never told Emily that I was there the night she got her diploma. I wasn't in the actual stadium. I was watching behind the fence, cursing myself out for all the right reasons. At the beginning I wanted to help her every time she was sad. All I wanted her to do was smile and feel better. But as I got closer to her, we started telling each other everything: every dream, every ghost, and every fear that was unwanted. She told me she loved me and I told her that I loved her too. I loved this person whose name is now in replay at my old school; that's the track, around the football field where I first saw her run. I'm outside the stadium because now it's her graduation. I hear her name play a thousand times before I bash my head with my hand for being such a fucking hellion.

Can anybody out there help me catch up? Help me learn how to be like you. I need to learn my lessons. Please, save me from loving everything...

Blood is on the fence because I don't know I have cut myself. I look at the dripping, the dropping of an amalgam of red, compressed in this plasma that's supposed to be traveling around my body and delivering nutrients and oxygen, but here it's about to fall on the cold cement; how fucking useless. "Deny gravity! Deny fucking gravity!" Only if that drop of blood was used for something else somehow, in some other time, some other place, maybe I'd be in a different universe, cheering with her family; just like she did for me.

`You fuck! If you don't want blood to spill, turn your`
`hand! Ever wonder how you got from one place to`
`another? You haven't, because you've always thought`
`that space moved for you. Everything moves for this`
`arrogant, selfish kid who thinks the universe is his.`
`This dimension you're sitting in is somewhere you don't`
`want to be. There are paper airplanes, made of cash`

money, flying everywhere you look. You're tripping on bronze coins, silver coins. All of these dead presidents have never been so alive. They're beating you with chairs and table legs every time you try to get up because you expect them to shower you with all the spoils of the world. So, you think you can make things happen for all these girls in your bed. You lay down next to mannequins whispering that you should close your eyes with them.

Next chance you get, listen to the sound that your time card at work makes when you punch it, and you'll hear a little laugh. Cause I know that your money is going to your spoiled baes who finger and fist their rotten cherries as you wait for one of them to be ready to pounce on top of you to squeeze out your Sundae ice cream, you self-centered little shit. Your mother is dying! Your mother is dying! Working, dying, working, dying.

I open my eyes and imagine where all the paychecks started. At some fast-food Asian restaurant with soda stained floor and cheap plastic chopsticks. I'm here, as a customer, talking to my slave self. He doesn't recognize me, I don't recognize me. There's no recognizing me because there is no me. Someone cooks the orders while someone keeps the tables clean. I imagine with hateful eyes, looking at myself throw away uneaten food. Throw away richness. Throw away carelessness. Then, wipe and clean the fucking tables. Disrespectful tables. Inconsiderate tables. God damn spoiled tables.

Money is good. It's not evil. It's only bad because people don't have any—money is good. You were born in a world designed where money is good. Money is freedom. Freedom to explore. Freedom to taste. Freedom to love. Money is good. It's laughable to think that money is bad. Money is good. Everyone needs to breathe. We all get it. A child doesn't need a book or a calculator to feel hunger. A child needs to eat. Desperation needs to feed. And you need to be able to afford to pay attention. Ignore your own hunger's protest for one night, and feed the child you let rot!

*Now, who am I? What am I? I'll go first with my public
introduction.*

I'm inside this little blue room, dying with a flaming fever. I'm here, burning
my own sweat. The closet light is on; the bathroom door is slightly open. There's
nothing here but shadows, and whoever let the devil in.

*I'm the sad little thing your mother couldn't suppress—
the evil and cruel memories you and her constantly run
across with.*

This is an evil idea. I don't know how to keep going, or whether I should. I've
never seen a ghost in my entire life, and I don't think this is one. But if I ever
did see a ghost, I promised myself that I'd talk to it; to run just feeds me hope
that I can lose it somehow—but there's no losing ghosts—there's no losing guilt
and regret.

     *"So, little child. Let's get to know each
other."*
     "You're a fucking bully."
     *"What? You're the bully. Anyone who reads this,
listen to what I'm telling you: don't feel bad for
this fucker; he a self-made lover of life who doesn't
know what the fuck life even is.*

Are you ready? Count with me! One, two, weee!"

*I don't know what's about to happen... but I think I know what's going to
happen... I don't think it's going to happen... but I fucking know it's going to...*

I hear a knock on the door. I hold my phone and the tears even more. It opens.
It's a figure, familiar to the heart, but not to the senses. It's Cecily. *Coming to
check-up on me?* She slowly walks towards the bed and I can see a faint smile
in the dark. Or, I felt it. I don't know. She sits on the bed and asks if I'm okay.
I'm shaking and I feel so wasted. There's no control anymore. I open myself up,
showing her everything: the writings, the analysis, the drama, everything. She
tells me it's okay. She tells me she understands. But I'm still not happy. I know
there's something missing. *Why does the demon keep coming back? Why does
this Creature keep creeping on my everything? I don't know, but I give up. I
finally let it take over.*

"Oh, my god! What the fuck are you doing!? Can you stop using Times New Roman and get the fuck back here with me? Stop trying to escape. Cecily's not even here with us. Stop trying to trick yourself of what's real and what's not! She doesn't even give a shit about you! She doesn't know where the fuck you are! You don't even know where you are! Stop listening to bullshit suggestions your little boy mind has made up, thinking that she cares... I should be writing a self-help guide, but this poet's powers don't extend down, down inside your self-hell. Here, there is no self-hell guide. The best thing I can do is instruct you to slap your own face with your dick and tell you, 'you're supposed to be a rational being too, not the other side of you that you keep feeding me. If I didn't run around your mind all the time I'd be fat from all the emotional shit you eat! Get with it! I'm your great interrogator, constant check-ups with an internal psychoanalyzator until you die—stay in this font. Stare at the words and you'll see that this is your typeface. This is where non-fiction accepts itself for what it is, where fiction holds hands with not. This is where you belong."

I grit my necklace tightly with my teeth, tripping in this deep chasm of a pause.

"Wow, nothing? Nothing?! Not even a little mood swing? Please go ahead and do nothing. Blame your friends, your parents, your environment, your gods. And just like him, her, and everybody who tried, you will be crucified, and nailed with a swing on your neck. You'll be in your casket wishing you were back in your birth basket, staring with an earthly blanket under the black stars of everything you've wished for.

I want to talk to you about another thing. If Cecily, or Gabrielle, or Emily, have no hold of you, you drunk booger-face, then why don't they know all about the pages of your story? Go all the way bitch, you fucking phony! Express the things people leave unsaid since you like trying to find honesty in dishonest objects!

Wait I thought... Why'd you stop talking? I thought, I thought..." the voice shifted to a flora's sense of touch. The harshness became petals, soft like the way Gabi would call out my name. *"... You wanted to be the lyrical poet? I'll be your pet poet by your side in a leash or in a bowl, you could fish me up like old man Santiago, from the sea of sentences, just for your own liking! Haha! —just kidding! Admit it! I am the corner. You are the tear. You are the conquered, I am your fear...! Let me tell you something! This battle in your head: It's just you thinking! It's not that big of a deal! But you're romanticizing it, you're dramatizing it! You're placing me in the ceiling, next to your ear, whenever you want me near, even though I clearly am not. And while that's happening, you make excuses for your little self to make sense of the world. Leave this fucking world! Get with that third person P-O-V like the first porn video you saw! First person narrator doesn't know shit!*

You don't know shit about everyone else. Did you even consider No L's feelings? You just deemed her as immature, when you shouldn't have felt annoyed or angry. You should feel bad about the good-girl because the Girlgod is so fucking strong in that one. Her condition eats her everything, like how a toddler eats its own shit. Just like how you eat your own—how about Cecily's feelings? Or Gabi's, or Emily's? Did you consider it hard enough? Or, are you still like little boy you, sitting on his bike, fixated on these wounded birds? —man, the world is bored of you. How sad is the world you live in that you who try so hard to seize understanding of it is still so far out of touch with the thing closest to you most! Who are you? You're a fucking no one. How do you expect to be responsible with other's feelings when you're so irresponsible with yourself?

Your friends don't even believe in you. They laugh, they joke. They're scared too and they're placing their fear in you. Brushing you off cause you act so god damn optimistic. You have this dream of doing good, you have ambitions meant only for gods, but you're a no one! How does a no one do good? Do no one types of things? The fuck is that? —aw what the fuck? Really? Teardrops on your phone? Really? Wah! Wah! Wah!

Cue the romantic orchestra, you're a fucking mess... Dan! Da! Whoosh! Rah! Listen to the strings, brass, wind, and bass that form this gargantuan piece of music climbing from a forte up to a fortissimo. Here comes the divulging crescendo! Bam! I commend you for thinking of leaving a message for Gabi, dunked and dipped in sin. You should call her and talk about Cecily and Emily. Tell her everything! —Hey! Do you think Cecily's on him? You know, right now? They're probably on a bed room, alone in church. Take me to her hosiery, down to the unholiest of all..."

"I need to deal with you first, you vulgar fuck!"

"Ooh, feisty. Boohoo, I'm such a potty-mouth. Cry me a flood! —Hey! You should ask other people to talk to me, to talk to themselves. They'll probably learn something different. They would actually hear what they think, and hear all the bullshit that they shit out of their mouth before they say it. Disrespect. Anger. You got no choice. I'll always be here. If you ever get your little book published. I'll be in those pages, in the margins, in the printed ink. That's when you're gonna go to me and indulge in my sick shit — You're funny. You always try to get rid of me. You keep stepping on that black uncomfortable thumbtack stabbing your heel. But still, I'm the best gift that you can always lose yourself in, always present, wrapped into your name that's not mentioned in this goddamn book..."

"I've killed you long ago... You've been dead to me, this whole time... I killed you the first time I yelled at my mother when I was nine. I killed you when I took the knife from my twelve-year-old sister's hand in the kitchen at fourteen years old. I killed you when I shared to Cait and stayed true to myself, no matter how much I got shit on for trying to be an honest un-gentleman. I killed you when I separated with Emily—three years and three months and fourteen days. It's so easy to break girls' hearts... Now I've broken the spell I had on her. I love her even now. I love her so much that I still cry about it, but it's okay—I killed you a long time ago... I killed you every single time I decided to do what I thought was the right thing to do—and Gabrielle... I need to call her now. I need to tell her I'm..."

"Not sorry for interrupting but, are you done? I'm still here... Congratulations... What do you think you are now?"

"A man who..."

"Amen, woo...? Amen, woo? Are you concluding this prayer to me with a little celebratory whimper? Hahaha! Oh no, not yet... You need me! You need someone to tell you that you made mistakes! I'm the little boy who yelled at your mother. I'm the little boy who feared losing his sister to the blade of suicide. I'm the one who wrote about Cecily on November 14, 2014. That was the day it would have been four years with Emily! Your book says the 15th of November because you keep lying to yourself. Fuck you! I'm the one who disrespected her. I'm the one who's going to fix it. I'm the one who destroyed everything! And I'm the one self-prescribed to heal everything—and now, I'm the one who's ignoring Gabrielle, and I'm the one who's *going to give her attention and mean it. I told her that she was immature. Still with her blankets and her mittens... riding her tricycle... I told her to hate every boy and girl in high school, to hate her father for not being a good father. Such a shame, she still cries about it... And I spoke so well and so sweet that she followed—she'd forgotten about me only when you came into the picture for the first time, but I have her again—Listen! Listen to me very, very carefully. LISTEN! LISTEN! LISTEN! I'm the one who loves! I'm the one who kills! I'm the one who writes. I'm the one who wrongs. And it's time to grow up... I'm going to make you weep, cause you're the little boy. I'm going to cry you out of my name! The name that's consumed your real name! I am! I am! I am! I am ashamed of you! Accept my invite so you can ascend from this purgatorial fulcrum. Do not waste my shame! Tame the roar of Cold Wind. Make your choice between two kinds of forever! No more silence. No more words. No more eyes. No nothing! Philosophy is dead without Sanity! Love loves nothing but itself! Receive it! Accept it...! Only then can the Poet help you..."*

... I'm dead... this is a monster I wasn't ready to write.

"HAHAHAHAHAHAHAHA...! YES! GOOD! THIS IS GOOD! WELCOME! WELCOME...! TO THE BOYGOD's PLAYGROUND. WELCOME. TO YOUR PLAYGROUND. OUR PLAYGROUND. WELCOME EVERYTHING! ABSOLUTELY EVERYTHING THAT COMES ALONG WITH IT...."

Mobile-Gabrielle Pilar-Call. *Ring! Ring! Ring! Ring! Ring! Ring!*
    "Hi! What's going on? Are you... okay...? You're breathing hard."
    "I'm sorry about everything. I didn't mean to do all of this. Especially not to you, well not just you, but many others. I just want to figure things out. "
    "What do you mean? Figure out what? Hey! Are you okay?"
    "No! Are you okay? Did he hurt you again!?"
    "Who hurt me—? My dad? Oh, no. I'm okay right—"
    "I think I'm having a manic attack...! I'm so, so sorry when I never—"
    "You're... up. Can't hear you... Hello? Hello...?" **–End Call.**

Signal failed. Agh! Piece of—hm... this must be good. This must be a gift. I don't want anyone knowing about this yet. But they will... oh god, they will.

When I was a young boy in the Philippines... I learned from church, watched from the evening *teleseryes*, and absorbed from everyone around me that loving people well is a fulfilling way of living. I was a *barrio-boy romantico*. I looked at myself at seven years old and knew that I was made to serenade. And so, I set myself to sing and care for that one beautiful person I end up falling in love with. But something started not making any sense as I grew up. Why did I want to sing to every beautiful thing with faces and features I can describe endlessly? I began to ache as I tried to find reasons as to why I'm told to Love well yet have to learn to suppress? Monogamy prevailed and I mistook it for a universal law. I'm different. I learned to love, different. And I want to say it... I want to release it. I don't want to be afraid anymore. Because out of anything in this universe, somehow this consciousness, this mind came to be. And its mine. Only mine. As it learned and learned, it began to feel more and more. And it learned that it doesn't want to keep these feelings left inside when I become once again nothing; I don't want to lay in Death's embrace leaving the Cosmos inside my brain unfulfilled. You don't have to be like me. You don't have to love the same way I do. But just like me, you also came to be. That is all the reason you and I need to evolve away from limitation. To be is our only permission for expression. I can see nothing that can take that away. And if there is, I say to that with the Fallen Angel in my tongue: I am authority. I am consent. I. am. permission.

I set my phone aside putting an end to dissecting my dramatis personae. I shake my head and think to myself. *Permission. Who are you kidding? You still have to ask for permission. From who? From what? From the world? From God...?* "Hey! Hey God...! I'm just... I'm just gonna lay dead here for a while... Is that, okay with you? Hm. Hello? Hello...? Are you there...? No? It's not okay then? Huh... okay, good—it's never been your choice anyway..." ... *zzz...*

I woke up to mother falling asleep frustrated today. She came from a graveyard shift and immediately crashed on the couch. I wouldn't have minded being left in peace, but I still had to get up.

Breakfast was left over chicken from last night; I was glad I saved it for today. "Did you two already eat?" I learned then that my sisters don't eat breakfast. I said okay and we left for school. Miel was first then Yanie was second. They both hurried out of the car, pressed by time. I told them to behave and be careful—there's truly nothing left to do after that—I went back to bed when I got home.

The sun's unusual heat in this January afternoon woke me up as sweat ran down my face. The time was an hour before school. I thought I've wasted so many moments that could be, but I didn't mind—and I enjoyed sleep; it was a smooth ride. It was as smooth as the drive from home to my academic life; no one dared to pray to danger and chance. Before I left the parking lot, I received a text invite to a party tonight. I respectfully replied a no.

Hands were shaken and hugs were given inside air conditioned classes that never left until our return. I saw Professor before I left work. But he didn't see me sitting in that same cobalt table I was a couple months ago.

The winds violently swayed my car, to and fro, during the highway ride. The swing reminded me of my current mood. I parked and watched the Ocean Side Mountains for a brief second. I didn't know why, but I didn't mind being late for work. No L welcomed me with a smile as I stepped into the facility. I didn't question it. I smiled back as I clocked in. I came early today to cover for Charlotte's class. The students were nice and none of them complained. I was grateful, but I didn't say. My classes were good and the kids had fun. I had fun. I was happy. I am happy. And because of all of this joy from everyone, the boys got to experience the tumble track. I made sure to make time; I thought they deserved it. "Name a strong animal!" I yelled loud and clear.

"Elephants!"

"Oh, um, dogs."

"Lions!"

"Okay, I'm going with lions," I told them. "When we do our tuck jumps, we bring our knees all the way up to the chest. That's what strong lions would do—wait! Everyone freeze! One at a time at the tumble track! You know the rules, come on!" The first boy in line stared at me as he bounced patiently up and down. I nodded to signify a go. "When you're done, go down towards the right side onto the floor and hug the tumble track! Watch out for other groups and team. Be very careful!"

"Ow! Ow!" a little student of mine cried out. I took a breath and asked Maddie and Nicole to watch my group behind me as I walked towards the boy. "Ow! It hurts!"

"Hey! Hey! Look at me!" I smiled and lifted my eyebrows. "Look at me. What color is your shirt?"

"Uh, red…" His eyes were watering milky tears.

"What color is… hey? I know your mom is over there, look at me for now. What color is your hair?"

"Brown." He settled down after a few deep breaths. I saw his mother from the corner of my eye try to extend comfort but all she could do was watch.

"Look at me and breathe with me." I looked at my other kids on the line intermittently. "Hey guys give me one second, okay!" I shouted at them. "Here I'll have you sit down for a minute, alright?" I set him up on the yellow edge of the tumble track. "Boys! Keep going, you're still in class. Be careful where you land. You're big boys now." The other boys continued on with the regimen. "You guys are what? Seven? Ten? Come on, you guys are tough." The little boy calmed down. "Come on dude you're tough. Let me see your biceps!" He flexed and I punched it with my pinkie. "See look at that, pain's gone—you want to get up with the line?" He nodded rapidly.

"Are you sure? It doesn't look like you're ready!"

"I'm ready!" A leviathan of a smile came about his face.

"Good! Get out of here and watch your step next time. Thank you for watching them," I said to Maddie and Nicole.

"Are you almost done at the tumble track?" Devon asked me while being dragged down by her over-the-top excited student.

"We're done now. You can have it."

"Thank you!" she said while trying to settle the girl next to her.

"Hey guys! Watch out for the other groups. Go get water! Watch your step! Guys! What did I say about baggy shorts and baggy pants?" Some lined up on the water fountain while some got their water bottles and dispensers from the bin. "Alright guys, we're done here. But first, let me see everyone lined up on the white line." I stood next to each of them. "Brian, good on your forward rolls, but you need to bring your hips up higher, and lean a little bit more—Jack, your front tuck is almost there! We just need the height! —Xavier, when you swing up the bar, hips up and quit it with the kicking— of the legs. But the swings are good and tight when you don't kick them! —Leo, how's your foot? Better?" He nodded. I nod in return. I gave each one of them a high five as I went along telling them what they needed to do. "Alright guys! Get outta here, I don't want to see you again! Just kidding! Go and thank your parents. Come back next week! We have more work to do!" I exchanged good nights with everyone but

Cecily and Cait. They don't work Thursday nights. But their spirits, along with my own, fade ever so slightly in the coach's corner.

"Coach Kati!" I raised my hand halfway to wave. She did the same.

"Oh, wait! You got a sec?" she called out. "Would you come tomorrow afternoon to the office? The office wants to ask if the guys shadowing you are ready to be on their own." I laugh at the thought of shadows.

"Yeah, I can do that. I have a morning class for Astronomy, so I'll come after." She said thank you as she walked passed me. A binder was put away. Lessons were learned. No lights were on. The office was closed. I exited out of the facility beneath a moonless sky.

I arrived home. My slippers were immediately put away. I prepared over-medium eggs for dinner and some garlic fried rice. I sat down to my hot meal and my cold milk. I said good night to the family and they do the same. After brushing my teeth, I fell on my bed ready for a recovery before the meeting tomorrow.

Writing felt foolish. But I indulged in it over and over again until the three in the morning dawn reminded me that unhealthy sleeping habits could one day kill me. The bed was closer to me now; we've both made friends with each other. I provided its purpose, while it gave me mine. I rested here and the four or nine-year-old, or any year old in me for that matter, looked at the clock. It was midnight. I got up with light feet and went through the small, condensed hallway.

I opened their door. There, they sleep like the baby I was; like the baby we all were. I kissed my sisters on the forehead keeping in my mind the things I want to give them; a good world I want them to live in. Then there was my mother sleeping like a child. "Good night *My*. I love you *po*." *Whatever nightmares you have, we'll all be here for you when you wake up. Mahal na mahal po namin kayo (We love you very much).*

I thought about my father; where he was, and where he could be. His job is four hours away; away from us again, like how it was when I was in the Philippines. But he comes back here every weekend just to see us. My heart felt that the man of the house wasn't here tonight. By the way I watched over my mother and sisters, I've never been so wrong.

Winter wasn't over; it was still so cold. So, I tucked myself inside my earthly blanket thinking I could sleep, but something in me took hold of my eyes. It spread nothing but flames. My head began to ache. It became harder to understand how a boy of seven years old, who once asked why he is who he is, is now twenty-one but still has no idea what is going on. *To be a man is to be what? Why can't I just know? Where is SPT? Guys, help! Heal me with a million messages! Remind me of the sound of how we all used to laugh.*

Don't cry, please; hush with the crying
right now. I know you're alone and I know
that you're scared. But the end of this
is the beginning; parallel worlds embrace
to bring heaven down to the hell you put
everyone in.

No more crying. Just take it all
out... the secrets of your logical,
insidious, and loving heart. Unleash
God's design upon your universe... so
finally, we can all be friends.

But if you're not enough to do
that—I WILL come back with someone else's
face, someone else's shape, someone with
the strength to himself name, and he or
she and I will try again, again, again,
again, over and over and over end over
end. until we're all friends.

For three hours, I recalled everything that happened. *Boygod's Playground*. I read it again and again, and cried like a baby calling out to his mother. The grey nightmare, the black bolts and lines, even the red hurt covered my entire mind.

Filipino boy. Getting pissed and annoyed, getting all Pinoyed. Letting all these Outsiders invade and settle in your heart. One comfortable bonfire and the imperial flames set loose. I'm sorry but cherub's arrows are too primal, too weak. History is fucking you all over again. And you need them to save you. Why? Why burden them with that? Aren't you enough...? Maybe not...

Agh! I love you all, but you all kill me. I need to take a break from all of you! I'm so generous and kind and this is what you do to me? I fucking hate all of you...! I'm inside my mind, my pages. All of it, mine alone! Mine! Mine! Mine! Mine! Mine! Mine! Mi—... Shut the fuck up! Shut up you little fucking kid! I'm sorry. Never mind me. I didn't mean for any of these things. I take it all back. I'm sorry that I've never done this before—being a man—I don't know what I'm doing. I don't know who or what I am—Cait. Cecily. Celebrate with ice cold drinks because all this is our beautiful choreography—Gabrielle. Your loving blush cradled me inside a forever that I've never been ready for—Emily. I...

I sat back on my bed and stared at the white ceiling. I looked at my stacked towers of books on my cabinet as it watched over me. All of the mementos from Emily and Gabrielle were happy: pendants, jars, letters, and captured moments with sacred pixels. Inside that heavenly moment, I kissed Gabrielle's necklace on my neck. Shortly thereafter, I smoothly followed through a natural thought. I took out Emily's plastic-sealed necklace within the depths of my wallet—and it was in this sentence that I realized I did nothing today but life.

> As a *barrio-boy romantico*, you live to write intimate lyrics; never feeling anything wrong with serenading anyone you want to love. But see baby boy, there *is* something wrong—there are those who would rather you keep your love to yourself. So, harden your heart by understanding: romantic love can't exist without someone else being unwanted. You. Her. Them. Us. We at some tragic point have to be the unwanted lover. That is a human condition. That is human non-fiction. And to escape this moral ruin, you have to play by the current rules. Study. Learn. One day, you'll find a way to be okay.

Nightmares... my most giving friends... it's way past midnight. Would you do your thing and take me away? Gently push my idle swing? Stop me from talking to myself, yeah? Let the Poet sleep. Please. Deliver me from all of my evil, and absolutely everything that comes along with it...

I heard a knock on the door. "Emily! Why are you here?" *I'm here to see you. Your mom let me in,* she told me. "But why? You told me never to speak to you anymore," I whispered back. *Just be nice and lay down.* So, I do as she said. *Is this another nightmare that hates me?* "Don't you hate me for everything I've done? For being the cause of our decay?" *Shhh... Nothing before or after matters right now,* she whispered. *Here... in this page... inside this sentence... There's only you... and how much you loved me... just say you loved me...* "You know I do..." *Deserting each other was our nightmare... but you... me... me...you... we were too far away... to do... anything.* I took my final breath awake. "Emily... you... were never the unwanted lover..." *I know... you were... Lyndon... zzz...*

BOYGOD

The End's Face

This is not a novel. It is a cluster fuck of such irresponsible intimate and romantic, yet necessary emotional expulsion that I didn't know what to do about... not until now.

Here we are. Done. recounting the phenomenon of psychological warfare. We can let it go.

But I must say this before we move on to greater things: the end of a prayer does not mean the end of the night. I know that the nightmares will come, and it wants to feed on the things we care about most—and inside these satanic replays, at the front of life's theater, is my little friend that will never leave; my little friend that sits alone under the light, while all of us are kept behind the curtains. I see that friend in you beneath every strain of logic, and every single insidious sin. Here. There. The face is everywhere. And after relying on some divine communication, thinking of it as nonsensical wishing, I thought I stopped praying, but I was wrong—no one is excused from worshiping and applauding the thing of the dark that we all kneel to in the end of our nightmares.

I hope for you to also befriend this thing that strangles the neck before caressing the cheeks. Release the Creature. Liberate the Poet. Don't ever let it sleep. Have no mercy in text and speech. Let the world be made mad by your Passions and your Spirit. This is the Human Want. Trust. Deliver the Art that is this Human Being. Only then will you find what God was looking for, before You and I came to be.

Amen.